Emily Brightwell is the pen name of Cheryl
Arguile. She is the author of the Mrs Jeffries murder
mystery series, and has also written romance novels
as Sarah Temple and Young Adult novels as Cheryl
Lanham. She lives in Southern California.

Visit Emily Brightwell's website at
www.emilybrightwell.com

D0635426

Also by Emily Brightwell
The Inspector and Mrs Jeffries
The Ghost and Mrs Jeffries
Mrs Jeffries Dusts for Clues
Mrs Jeffries Stands Corrected
Mrs Jeffries on the Ball
Mrs Jeffries Takes Stock
Mrs Jeffries Plays the Cook
Mrs Jeffries and the Missing Alibi
Mrs Jeffries Takes the Stage
Mrs Jeffries Questions the Answer
Mrs Jeffries Reveals Her Art
Mrs Jeffries Takes the Cake
Mrs Jeffries Weeds the Plot
Mrs Jeffries Pinches the Post
Mrs Jeffries Pleads Her Case
Mrs Jeffries Sweeps the Chimney
Mrs Jeffries Stalks the Hunter
Mrs Jeffries and the Silent Knight
Mrs Jeffries Appeals the Verdict
Mrs Jeffries and the Best Laid Plans
Mrs Jeffries and the Feast of St Stephen
Mrs Jeffries Holds the Trump
Mrs Jeffries in the Nick of Time
Mrs Jeffries and the Yuletide Weddings
Mrs Jeffries Speaks Her Mind
Mrs Jeffries Forges Ahead
Mrs Jeffries and the Mistletoe Mix-Up
Mrs Jeffries Defends Her Own

Mrs Jeffries Rocks the Boat

Emily Brightwell

CONSTABLE

CONSTABLE

First published in the US in 1999 by The Berkley Publishing Group,
an imprint of Penguin Group (USA) Inc.

This edition published in Great Britain in 2018 by Constable

1 3 5 7 9 10 8 6 4 2

A CIP catalogue record for this book
is available from the British Library.

ISBN 978-1-47212-561-3

Typeset in Bembo by TW Type, Cornwall
Printed and bound in Great Britain by CPI Group (UK) Ltd, Croydon CR0 4YY
Papers used by Constable are from well-managed forests and
other responsible sources

MIX
Paper from
responsible sources
FSC® C104740

Constable
An imprint of
Little, Brown Book Group
Carmelite House
50 Victoria Embankment
London EC4Y 0DZ

An Hachette UK Company
www.hachette.co.uk

www.littlebrown.co.uk

CHAPTER ONE

Malcolm Tavistock unlocked the heavy, spiked gate and pushed it open. 'Come along, Hector,' he said, yanking gently on the bulldog's lead. Hector, with one last sniff at an errant dandelion that had poked up between the stone squares of the footpath, followed his master.

'Humph,' Tavistock glared at the dandelion as he and the dog stepped into the gated garden in the middle of Sheridan Square. He made a mental note to have a word with the gardener. The place certainly looked scruffy. He pulled the gate shut behind him and made sure he heard the lock engage before carefully pocketing the key.

Sheridan Square was for residents only. It wasn't a public garden and Malcolm, for his part, would do his best to insure it never became one. It rather annoyed him that some of his other neighbors on the square weren't as diligent as he was about insuring the security of the garden. Tugging at the dog's lead, Tavistock strolled up the footpath toward the center of the large square, his eagle eye on the lookout for more signs of neglect on the part of the gardener. The animal trudged along next to his master, keeping his nose close to the ground and sniffing happily at the bits of grass and clumps of leaves.

Suddenly, Hector came to a dead stop and his thick white head shot up. He sniffed the air and then lunged up the path, yanking his master along behind him.

'Hold on, old fellow,' Malcolm ordered as he pulled back on the lead. He wasn't through ascertaining exactly how much of a tongue-lashing to give that wretched gardener. 'Humph,' he sniffed as he surveyed the area. The place was abysmal. The bushes along the perimeter had grown high and unwieldy. The footpath was scattered with stems and leaves and bits of dried grass, the flower beds were filled with weeds, and the lilac bushes were completely overgrown. 'Well, really,' Malcolm muttered. 'Am I the only one that cares how this garden looks? The garden committee shall certainly hear about this.'

Hector lunged again, almost yanking Malcolm off his feet.

'Oh, all right.' Malcolm finally decided to let the poor dog have his walkies. He looked around, saw that he was the only one in the garden, and then dropped the lead. 'Go on, boy. I'll catch up in a moment.' Hector took off like a shot. Malcolm reached down and picked up a dirty bit of paper that was littering the path. 'Honestly,' he muttered as he crumpled the paper into a tight ball, 'some people have no consideration for others.'

From the center of the square, Hector howled.

Malcom was so startled, he jumped. He stuffed the

paper in his pocket and ran towards his dog. His heart pounded against his chest. For all his grumbling, he loved that silly dog, and Hector might look like a terror, but he was easily upset.

Flying up the path, Malcolm skidded to a halt. Hector was perfectly all right. He was standing next to a bench upon which a woman lay stretched out sound asleep.

'Well, really,' he exclaimed. 'What has become of this neighborhood! Hector, come away from that disreputable person immediately.' This wasn't the first time such a thing had happened. Because the garden was shielded by the high foliage from the eyes of passing policemen, vagrants occasionally climbed the fence. But this was the first time Malcolm had ever seen a woman do it. 'What is the world coming to?' Malcolm muttered. He marched toward the bench. 'I blame those silly suffragettes,' he told Hector. 'Puts stupid ideas in women's heads.' He bent over the sleeping woman, frowning as he realized her clothes were new and expensive. Not the sort of clothes a vagrant would wear. He was suddenly a bit cautious. 'Uh, miss.' He poked her gently in the arm. 'Is everything all right?'

The woman lay silent.

Hector whined softly.

Frightened now, Malcolm looked around him at his surroundings and wished he were visible from the street. The hair on the back of his neck stood up, and he shivered. But he couldn't just leave the woman lying here. 'Miss,' he said loudly, 'are you all right?'

Hector whined again and stuck his nose under the

3

wooden slats. But his head wouldn't go in very far as the lead had got tangled around the base of the gas lamp next to the bench. Malcolm bent down and untangled the lead; as he stood up, he saw what was under the bench. Stunned, he blinked and then forced himself to look again. But the view didn't change. In the pale morning light it was easy to see exactly what it was. Blood. Lots of it. Grabbing the dog's lead, he pulled him hard toward the gate. 'Come on, Hector, we've got to find a policeman. That poor woman's dead. There's blood everywhere.'

Hepzibah Jeffries, housekeeper to Inspector Gerald Witherspoon of Scotland Yard, stepped into the kitchen and surveyed her kingdom with amusement. Wiggins, the apple-cheeked young footman, sat at the kitchen table. Beside him sat a scruffy young street arab named Jeremy Blevins. In front of them was an open book, a pencil and a large sheet of paper. At the far end of the long table, Betsy, the blond-haired maid, sat polishing silver. Mrs Goodge, the gray-haired, portly cook stood at the kitchen sink scrubbing vegetables for the evening stew.

The only one missing was Smythe, the coachman. But as it was almost morning teatime, Mrs Jeffries expected him in any minute.

'Shall I make the tea?' Mrs Jeffries asked the cook as she came on into the kitchen.

'No need.' Mrs Goodge jerked her chin to her left, toward a linen-covered tray that rested on the counter. 'It's all done. But if you could just put the kettle on to boil, I'd be obliged. My hands are wet.'

4

'Certainly.' The housekeeper did as she was asked.

'Come on now, Jeremy,' Wiggins said to the lad, 'Concentrate. You know what that letter is. You learned it yesterday.'

'I am concentratin',' the boy shot back. 'But it's bloomin' hard to remember every little thing.' His thin face scrunched as he stared at the book. 'Uh, it's a V,' right?'

'It's a "G",' Wiggins corrected. 'Can't you remember?'

'Leave off, Wiggins,' Betsy interjected. 'Jeremy's doing well. He's learned ever so much in just a few days.'

'Ta, miss.' Jeremy beamed at Betsy. 'I reckon I've done well too . . . mind you, I don't know why I'm botherin' with book learnin'. It's not like the likes of me'll ever get a chance to use it much.'

'You don't want to be ignorant all yer life, do ya?' Wiggins cuffed the lad gently on the arm and closed the book. 'Besides, you never know what the future holds. At least if you know your letters and can read a bit, you'll be able to sign your own name.'

'Fat lot of good that'll do me,' Jeremy grumbled. He'd only told this lot he wanted to learn to read as a means of getting into the house and having a bite of food every now and again. He'd not expected they'd take him at his word and whip out this silly book every time he came around because his belly was touching his backbone. Still, Jeremy mused, they were a decent lot. Treated him well, even if they did expect him to learn his bleedin' letters. He glanced at the covered tray and wondered what sort of goodies were under the linen. He'd already been fed, but it never hurt to get some extra. When you lived like he did, you never knew when you might next eat. 'Are ya havin' a fancy tea, then?'

'No,' Betsy replied. She tossed her polishing cloth to one side and stood up. 'Just our usual. Why? Are you still hungry?' Having been raised in one of the poorest slums of London, she was well aware of what the lad was up to. She'd lived on the streets for a time herself and knew what it was like to try and survive. 'Help yourself to some more buns if you're still feeling peckish. There's plenty in the larder.' She lifted the heavy tray of silver and started for the pantry.

Surprised, Jeremy gaped at her and then quickly scrambled to his feet. He didn't bother to look at the others; he simply followed Betsy down the hallway. He'd known as soon as he asked the question that he should have kept his mouth shut. When people were doling out charity, they didn't like you to be greedy. He couldn't believe she wasn't cuffing him on the ears or giving him a lecture.

'The buns are in the dry larder,' Betsy called over her shoulder. She indicated a closed door she'd just passed and grinned as she heard it creak open behind her.

'Thanks, miss,' Jeremy called as he darted inside the larder. 'I'll 'elp meself if ya don't mind.'

At the far end of the hall, the back door opened and a tall, dark-haired fellow with heavy features stepped inside. He took one look at the maid and frowned ominously . . . it was a scowl that could send strong men running for cover, but it had no effect whatsoever on Betsy. 'You oughtn't to be lift-in' that 'eavy tray.' He came forward and took it out of her hands.

'Don't be silly, Smythe,' she replied. 'It's not at all heavy. It's only a bit of silver.'

Smythe, the coachman, had been courting Betsy for some time now. Though they seemed quite mis-matched, they were, in fact, very devoted to one another. He glanced up the hall to make sure the coast was clear and then leaned forward and snatched a quick kiss.

Jeremy chose that moment to pop out of the pantry. 'I only took . . .' His voice trailed off as the two adults sprang apart.

Betsy whirled about, her face crimson at having been caught, even by a street lad. 'Did you get some buns, then?'

Jeremy, who was almost as embarrassed as the maid, held up two of them. He'd been tempted to take more but decided against it. 'I took these for me sister,' he explained honestly. 'She's only four. I'd best be off then,' he mumbled as he pushed past the couple and headed for the back door, 'Tell Wiggins I'll be back in a couple of days,' he said as he scurried out and slammed the door behind him.

'I do think we embarrassed the boy.' Smythe's voice was amused.

'You shouldn't have kissed me,' Betsy hissed. 'He'll tell Wiggins, you know.'

Smythe only grinned. The entire household knew that he and Betsy were sweethearts. Knew and approved. But unfortunately, their courtship kept getting interrupted by the inspector's murder cases. 'Help me take this to the pantry,' he said softly.

'You don't need any help,' Betsy protested. She looked quickly back toward the kitchen. 'The others will wonder what we're up to.'

'The others will understand we're doin' a bit of courtin',' he insisted. He started for a closed doorway opposite the wet larder.

'All right.' Betsy followed him. 'What have you been doing this morning?'

He opened the pantry door and stepped inside. 'After I dropped the inspector off, I took Bow and Arrow for a good run,' he replied. 'They needed the exercise. Where do ya want this?'

'Put it over there.' Betsy pointed to an empty shelf on the opposite wall. The tiny butler's pantry was too small for furniture. It consisted mainly of shelves of various sizes running up and down the length of the walls. Smythe carefully eased the tray into its place and then turned and pulled her close in a bear hug. Betsy giggled.

In the kitchen, Wiggins glanced toward the hallway. 'I thought I 'eard Smythe come in.' He started to get up. 'And where's that lad got to?'

'Sit down, Wiggins,' Mrs Jeffries ordered. 'Smythe has come in, and I think he's probably helping Betsy put the silver away. I expect that Jeremy has helped himself to some buns and left.' Unlike the footman, she knew precisely what was going on down the hallway.

'But I need to 'ave a word with Smythe.' Wiggins started to get up again. ''E promised to . . .'

8

'Sit down, boy,' Mrs Goodge said sharply. 'You've no need to go botherin' Smythe now. He'll be in for his tea in a few minutes. You can talk to him then.'

'But Betsy's talkin' to 'im now . . .' Wiggins's voice trailed off as he realized what the two women already knew. His broad face creased in a sheepish grin. 'Oh, I see what ya mean. They're doin' a bit of courtin'.'

'That's none of our business.' Mrs Goodge placed the tray of food in the center of the table. She pushed a plate of sticky buns as far away from Wiggins as possible and shoved a plate of sliced brown bread and butter in front of the boy. He ate far too many sweets. Then she put the creamer and sugar bowl next to the stack of mugs already on the table. Lastly, she put the heavy, brown teapot in front of the housekeeper and then shoved the empty tray onto the counter behind her.

Mrs Jeffries smiled her thanks and began pouring out the tea. She'd done a lot of thinking about Betsy and Smythe. They were, of course, perfect for one another. She certainly hoped that Smythe would ask the girl to marry him. She wasn't foolish enough to think a change of that significance wouldn't have an effect on the household. It would. A profound effect.

To begin with, she wondered if the two of them would want to stay on in the household if they married. Normally, a maid and a coachman who wed would simply move into their own room and stay on. But these weren't normal circumstances. Smythe would want to give his bride her own home. A home she suspected he could well afford. The housekeeper was fairly certain that one of the main reasons he'd

9

not yet proposed was because he couldn't think of a way to tell the lass the truth about himself. But that wasn't what was worrying the housekeeper. Smythe could deal with that in his own good time. What concerned her was what would happen to their investigations if Smythe and Betsy married and moved out.

She sighed inwardly. There was nothing constant but change in life, she thought. When she'd come here a few years back, she'd never thought she and the others would get so involved in investigating murders. But they had. They'd done a rather good job of it as well, she thought proudly. Not that their dear inspector suspected they were the reason behind his success as Scotland Yard's most brilliant detective. Oh dear, no, that would never do.

Mrs Jeffries put the heavy pot down. They'd come together and formed a formidable team. The household, along with their friends Luty Belle Crookshank and her butler Hatchet had investigated one heinous crime after another. Those investigations had brought a group of lonely people closer to one another. In their own way, they'd become a family. Now they had to make some adjustments. Murder, as interesting as it was, couldn't compete with true love. Especially, she told herself, when they didn't even have one to investigate. Not that she was thinking that someone ought to die just so she and the rest of the staff could indulge themselves. Goodness, no, that would never do. Murder was a terrible, terrible crime. It was impossible to think otherwise.

Still, if someone did die, she thought wistfully, it would break the monotony of the household routine and give all of them a much-needed bit of excitement. She shook herself when she realized where her thoughts were taking her. Then she looked up and found the cook gazing at her with an amused expression on her face. There were moments, Mrs Jeffries thought, when she was sure Mrs Goodge could read her mind.

'Mr Tavistock, if you'll just tell us how you came to find the body, please,' Inspector Gerald Witherspoon said gently to the portly, well-dressed gentleman.

'Yes, I will, just give me a moment, please.' He swallowed and glanced down at the fat bulldog that sat at his feet, seeming to take strength in the animal's presence. He lifted his head and ran a hand nervously through his wispy gray hair. His blue eyes were as big as saucers, and his elderly face was pale with shock.

Inspector Witherspoon, a middle-aged man with thinning dark hair, a fine-boned, pale face and a mustache, smiled kindly at the witness he was trying to interview. The poor fellow was so rattled, the hands holding the dog's lead trembled. Witherspoon didn't fault the man for being upset. Finding a corpse generally had that effect on people. To be perfectly frank, it still rattled him quite a bit.

'I've already told those constables.' Tavistock pointed a shaky finger at two uniformed police guarding the bench on which the body still lay. 'I don't think I ought to have to tell it again. It's most upsetting.'

'I'm sure it is, sir,' the inspector replied. He glanced at the policeman standing next to Tavistock.

11

Constable Barnes, an older, craggy-faced, gray-haired veteran who worked with Witherspoon exclusively, stared impassively out at the scene.

'Constable,' Witherspoon said, 'have one of the lads take Mr Tavistock home. We'll have a look at the body and then pop over and take his statement when we're finished.'

Tavistock slumped in relief. 'Thank you, Inspector. I live just across the Square.' He pointed to a large, pale gray home on the far side. 'I don't mind admitting I could do with a cup of tea.'

Barnes signaled to a uniformed lad, and a few moments later the witness, with his dog in tow, was escorted home. Witherspoon stiffened his spine and started up the footpath toward the body. He'd put off actually having to see it till the last possible moment. But he knew his duty. Distasteful as it was, he'd look at the victim.

He simply hoped it wasn't going to be too awful.

'She's right here, sir,' the PC standing guard called out as soon as he spotted the inspector. 'We did just like Constable Barnes instructed, we didn't touch anything.'

'Good lad.' Witherspoon swallowed heavily. He stopped next to the bench and looked down at the victim.

'She's not all that young,' Barnes murmured. He'd come back to stand at the inspector's elbow. 'And her clothes don't appear to be tampered with.'

'True,' Witherspoon replied. The victim was a middle-aged woman with dark brown hair peeking out of her sensible cloth bonnet. The hat skewed to the side revealed a few strands of gray at her temples. She wore a deep blue traveling dress with expensive gold buttons. Her feet, shod in black high button shoes, dangled off the end of the bench. 'She's tall,' Witherspoon muttered. 'That bench is over five and a half feet long.' For a moment, he forgot his squeamishness. Except for the blood pooling underneath the bench she could almost be asleep. Her skin hadn't taken on that hideous milk blue color he'd seen in other corpses. He rather suspected that meant she'd not been dead long.

'She's not got any rings on sir.' Barnes pointed to her hands, both of which were splayed out to one side of the body. 'So unless the killer stole them, I think we can assume she's not married.'

'But the killer may very well have stolen her jewelry,' the inspector said. 'As you can see, she's not got a purse or a reticule with her. Not unless it's underneath the body.'

Taking a deep breath, he squatted down next to her. Barnes did the same. 'Let's turn her over,' Witherspoon instructed. Gently, the two men turned her on her side. The inspector winced. 'She's been stabbed. I rather thought that might be the case.'

'Poor woman.' Barnes shook his head in disgust. 'And from the looks of that wound, it weren't a clean, quick kill either.'

Witherspoon forced himself to examine the wounds more closely. The constable was right, the woman's dress was in ribbons, and it was obvious, even to his untrained eye, that she'd been stabbed several times before she died.

'How many times do you reckon?' Barnes asked.

'It's impossible to tell. The police surgeon ought to be able to give us an answer after he's done the post mortem.'

'She might have screamed some,' Barnes said grimly. 'As it looks like the first thrust didn't kill her, maybe someone heard something.'

'Let's hope so,' Witherspoon mumbled. 'But I don't have much hope for that. There's a constable less than a quarter mile from here. Why didn't someone go get him if they heard a woman screaming?'

Barnes shrugged. 'You know how folks are, sir. Lots of them don't want to get involved.'

Together, they gently lowered the body back down. Witherspoon stared at the poor woman and offered a silent prayer for her. There was nothing more they could learn from her. She'd gone to her final rest in the most heinous, awful manner possible. Now it was up to him to see that her killer was brought to justice.

Witherspoon cared passionately about justice.

'There's nothing on her to identify her, sir.' Barnes stated. He stood up. 'Nothing in her pockets and no purse or muff.'

'Hmmm.' The inspector frowned heavily. 'We must find out who she is. Let's give the garden a good search. There may be a clue here. You know what I always say, Barnes, even the most clever of murderers leaves something behind.'

Barnes blinked in surprise. He'd never heard the inspector say anything of the sort. 'Right, sir.'

'We'd best send a lad back to the station to see if

there are reports of any missing persons matching the victim's description.'

'Right, sir.'

'And I suppose I ought to send a message home' – Witherspoon stroked his chin thoughtfully – 'and let them know I'm probably going to be late.' Drat. Tonight he'd planned on sitting in the communal gardens with Lady Cannonberry, his neighbor. But duty, unfortunately, must come before pleasure. 'You'd better let your good wife know as well, Constable. Can't have people worrying about us when we're late for supper.'

'I'll take care of it, sir.' Barnes replied with a grateful smile. He was touched by Witherspoon's thoughtfulness. His good wife would worry if he was late.

They spent the next half an hour searching the area, but even with the help of five additional policemen, they found nothing in the square that gave them any indication of who their victim might be.

When the body had been readied for transport to the morgue, Witherspoon and Barnes followed it out to the street. They left two constables inside to guard the area and also to keep an eye out for who came and went in this garden.

The attendants loaded her into the van and trundled off. Witherspoon turned to his constable. 'Right, we've a murder to solve, then. Let's get cracking. Send some lads around on a house to house to see if anyone heard or saw anything.' His gaze swept the area. 'I daresay, this is quite a nice area.'

'Very posh, sir,' Barnes replied. 'And the garden is private, sir. That ought to make it easier.' He pointed to the gate. 'You need a key to get inside. But there wasn't a key on the victim, so that means she either knew her killer and came in with him or her, or the gate was already unlocked when she got here.'

'I suppose she could have scaled the fence,' Witherspoon muttered. He looked at the high, six-foot spiked railings and then shook his head. 'No, that's not likely. Not a woman of that age.'

Barnes smiled. 'I agree, sir. I can't see her leaping the ruddy thing.'

'I suppose she could have had a key and the killer took it with him after he'd stabbed her,' Witherspoon said thoughtfully.

'The only people with keys are residents of the square,' Barnes said. 'Malcolm Tavistock said he'd never laid eyes on the woman before and he ought to know. He's lived here for years.'

'Who?'

'Tavistock,' Barnes replied. 'The man who found her.'

'Ah yes.' Witherspoon nodded sympathetically. 'Poor fellow. Finding a body isn't a very nice way to start one's day.'

'Neither is getting stabbed.'

'Right,' Witherspoon sighed. Sometimes he felt a bit inadequate for the task at hand. But then again, he'd try his very best. 'Let's get on with it. Where does Mr Tavistock live?'

'This way, sir.'

The Tavistock house was directly across from the entrance to the garden. Like its neighbors, the dwelling was a pale gray, three-story townhouse with a freshly painted white front door. The inspector banged the shiny gold knocker, and almost instantly Malcolm Tavistock stuck his head out. 'I suppose you want to come in?' he said grudgingly.

Witherspoon didn't take offense at the man's words. 'That would be helpful, sir,' he replied. He was inclined to give the poor fellow the benefit of the doubt. The shock of stumbling across a body could make someone behave in the most appallingly rude way.

Tavistock gestured for them to step inside. 'Hurry up, then. Let's get this over and done with. I've an appointment in a few moments.' He turned on his heel and stalked toward a set of open double doors off the foyer.

'I do beg your pardon, sir. But we'll need a complete statement,' Witherspoon said as he and the constable followed Tavistock. They came into a large drawing room. The decor was nicely done, but hardly opulent or unusual. The walls were painted a dark green and the windows covered with heavy gold damask curtains. A huge fireplace, over which hung the requisite portrait of an ancestor, dominated the far end of the room. Fringe-covered tables, bookcases and over-stuffed furniture completed the picture.

Tavistock flopped down on a mulberry-colored leather chair and gestured at the opposite settee. 'Do sit down, then. I'd offer you tea, but I've no staff at the moment.'

'You're here alone, sir?' Witherspoon asked. The house was large and well maintained. He'd be surprised if one person could take care of it alone.

'My servants aren't due back until tomorrow,'

Tavistock explained. 'They weren't expecting me home until the end of the week. I've been abroad.'

'On business, sir?' the constable asked. He'd taken out his notebook and flipped it open.

The inspector nodded approvingly at the constable's initiative. He encouraged Barnes to participate in questioning witnesses.

'Hardly. Frankly, I can't see that my reasons for being out of the country are anyone's business but my own. Now, can we please get on with this? As I said, I've an appointment in a few moments.'

The inspector sighed inwardly. He did wish that people were a tad more respectful of the police. It wasn't as if they came around disrupting people's lives because they'd nothing better to do. 'We'll try to be as quick as possible. Can you tell us precisely how you came to find the body?'

'I didn't find it,' Tavistock said. 'Hector did. He dashed off down the footpath and a few moments later, he was kicking up a terrible fuss. Not like him, he's generally such a good dog, quite well behaved.'

Hector, licking his chops, ambled into the drawing room at just that moment. He took one look at the two policemen, snorted in a loud, bulldog fashion and then trotted over and planted his rather large behind firmly next to his master's feet.

Witherspoon couldn't help smiling. He liked dogs. Mind you, he didn't think this one looked quite as intelligent as his own dog, Fred. But as Tavistock's expression had brightened noticeably at the animal's appearance, the inspector wisely kept his opinion to himself.

'What time was this, sir?' Barnes asked.

Tavistock thought for a moment. 'Let me see, usually I take Hector out for his walkies at seven every morning, but as we're a bit off our schedule, overslept as it were, I think it was closer to seven fifteen when we finally managed to get outside.'

Hector's head snapped up at the word 'walkies.' He whined softly. Tavistock reached down and absently patted him on the head. 'Now, now, old fellow, we'll go walkies later.'

'You went straight out your front door and directly into the garden, is that it?' Witherspoon asked. He'd learned it was most valuable to get time sequences sorted out correctly. He'd had some rather substantial success in the past solving crimes with the help of timetables.

Tavistock's thin eyebrows rose in surprise. 'Where else would I go? I was taking Hector for his morning walk. Of course I went straight from the house to the garden. Why would I pay a substantial amount of money each year for the upkeep of a private garden if I didn't use it?'

'We're only trying to establish all the facts, sir,' Barnes said smoothly. 'You left here at seven fifteen and went straight across? You didn't stop to talk with anyone?'

Tavistock nodded. 'There was no one to speak to, Constable. Seven fifteen is quite early.'

'Is the garden always locked?' Witherspoon asked.

'Always. We're most particular about that. Any resident that leaves it unlocked is subject to a fine.'

'I see.' The inspector nodded. 'And how many people have keys?'

Tavistock frowned thoughtfully. 'Well, there's seven houses on the square. Each household is issued a key of course . . . no, no, I tell a lie. Mrs Baldridge down at number one doesn't have one.'

'Why not?' The inspector asked.

'She did have one, but you see, she doesn't any-more. There was a terrible row over the hollyhocks.' He waved his hand dismissively. 'The woman simply couldn't get it through her head that the wretched flowers wouldn't grow properly in that soil. So the garden committee decided to plant something else. She was most upset. She chucked her key at us and told us to go to the devil.'

The inspector tried not to smile. 'But there are seven keys in existence, correct.'

'No, there's eight. The gardener has one, of course.' Tavistock crossed his legs and leaned back.

'Could you give us the names of the other residents?' Barnes asked.

Tavistock glanced pointedly at a clock on the top of a cabinet a few feet away from where he sat. He sighed. 'I'm going to be dreadfully late, Inspector. Can't we do this another time? Say this afternoon perhaps?'

'We're sorry to inconvenience you, sir,' Witherspoon explained. 'But the sooner we begin our investigation, the sooner we can get this sorted out.'

'All right.' Tavistock shrugged. 'Let's, see, there's Mrs Baldridge at number one. She's just across the square, but as I said, she had no key.'

'Who does have her key, sir?' Barnes asked.

Tavistock frowned thoughtfully. 'I'm not sure. Mr Heckston, I imagine. He's the head of the committee . . . yes, he's bound to have it. Mrs Baldridge was aiming at his head when she chucked the key. Quite a good aim for a woman her age. Smacked him right in the nose.'

Barnes ducked his head to hide a smile. 'And who else, sir?'

'Mrs Lucas at number two has a key.' He held up his fingers and ticked them off one by one as he spoke. 'The Heckstons at number three, Colonel Bartell at number four, the Prospers at number six . . .'

'Who's at number five?' Witherspoon asked.

'No one,' Tavistock said. 'The owner died last year and the place has been empty ever since. I believe the rest of the family are in India or Canada. Let's see now, where was I, oh yes. The Prospers, number six and lastly, there's me, of course. I live here at number seven.'

'There's only seven houses on the square.' Barnes could have sworn there were more than that.

'Oh yes.' Tavistock beamed proudly. 'The houses are all quite large, sir. Not like some other places I could mention. There's only the seven of us.'

'What's the gardener's name and where can I locate him?' Witherspoon asked. He was confident that Barnes had written down all the necessary particulars about the square's residents, and he wanted to make sure he took care of this bit of information before it completely slipped his mind.

'Jonathan Siler,' Tavistock said. 'I don't know

where he lives. You can get that information from Mr Heckston. But I'm sure that Jonathan hasn't anything to do with this poor woman's death. He's been taking care of the garden for years and he's a decent fellow, certainly wouldn't go about stabbing his betters. Not, of course, that we don't have to keep after him to keep the place up to our standards. You know how that class of person is. They'll do a fine job as long as you keep a close eye on them.'

Witherspoon said nothing. He could easily have argued the point. He'd seen more than one case of murder where someone's 'betters' got a bullet in the brain or a knife in their back. 'I'm sure your gardener is most trustworthy. But you do understand, we have to talk with him.'

'He's due here this morning,' Tavistock said. 'As a matter of fact, he ought to be turning up any moment now.'

'When did you arrive back from your trip abroad?' Witherspoon asked.

'Yesterday evening. I stopped and had a bite to eat in a restaurant near Victoria, fetched Hector and came on home.'

'And how long have you been gone, sir?' Barnes asked.

'Two weeks. I'd planned to stay longer.' Tavistock smiled sheepishly, 'but I found myself missing home.' Again he leaned down and patted his dog. 'You know how it is, sir. One goes off expecting to have a marvelous time and one finds that one misses the comforts of home. I know everyone says Italy has such superb weather, but frankly, this time of year it's simply too hot. I'd fully planned on staying a month. I sent the staff a telegram telling them I was coming home early.'

'I see,' Witherspoon said slowly. He didn't think there was much more this witness could tell him. Nodding at Barnes, he rose to his feet. 'You've been most helpful, sir. Pity you weren't in the garden last night . . .'

'Who says I wasn't?' Tavistock exclaimed. 'Of course I went into the garden. I had to take Hector walkies before we retired. Mind you, it was quite late when we went in, around midnight I should say.'

'Why were you there so late?' Barnes asked.

Tavistock shot him a disgruntled look. 'You obviously don't have a dog, Constable. Especially a dog that's quite excited to see you.'

'Oh.' The constable nodded in understanding. 'Took him out to do his business, I see.'

'Precisely, sir. We went all the way into the garden too.'

'And there was nobody there,' Witherspoon said.

'Precisely,' Tavistock replied. 'If there had been, Hector would have found them. He's quite good at finding things.'

CHAPTER TWO

Betsy broke into a welcoming smile as she opened the front door. 'Constable Griffiths, how nice to see you. What brings you here? Inspector Witherspoon was up and out hours ago.' She could tell by the pleased expression on his face that he hadn't come bearing bad news about their inspector.

'I've brought a message for the household, miss.' He smiled bashfully. 'Inspector Witherspoon's been called out on a murder case. He won't be home till quite late.'

'A murder. Really?' Betsy threw the door open wide. 'Come in, then.'

'I'd love to, Miss Betsy,' he explained, 'but I've got to get over to Constable Barnes's house and tell his missus he won't be home in time for supper.'

Betsy wasn't about to let the details of a murder slip through her fingers so easily. 'Oh, but you must have a cup of tea,' she implored him with a pouting smile. She hated using such tactics to get her own way, but she simply couldn't risk his going without telling them the details. 'You simply must. It's so warm out

24

today, I'm sure you're tired from coming all the way over here. Come down to the kitchen with me.'

Constable Griffiths hesitated. He was quite sweet on Miss Betsy. She was ever such a pretty girl. But he didn't wish to be derelict in his duty. 'I really shouldn't, miss.'

'Nonsense, if you're worried about getting the message to Mrs Barnes, don't be.' She reached out, snagged his arm and tugged him into the house. Surprised by her aggressiveness, he found himself inside before he could stop her.

'It's still quite early, you'll have plenty of time to get to the Barnes house.' Betsy slammed the door shut on her victim and gave him another dazzling smile. 'Inspector Witherspoon would be most upset if he knew we'd let you leave without giving you refreshment.' Still holding his arm, she tugged him towards her, whirled about and ran smack into Smythe.

He glared at the dainty hand on the constable's sleeve.

Betsy glared right back at him. 'Constable Griffiths's come to give us a message,' she blurted before Smythe could run the poor lad off. 'There's been a murder, and the inspector won't be home till late. We're just on our way to the kitchen to have tea.'

With the men in tow, Betsy led the way downstairs.

When the three of them trooped into the kitchen, Mrs Jeffries and Mrs Goodge, who were sitting at the table, making up menus for the week, looked up in surprise.

'There's been a murder,' Betsy blurted, 'and

Constable Griffiths's come all this way just to let us know the inspector'll be home late. I insisted he have a cup of tea before he goes on to the Barnes house.'

'But of course he'll have tea.' Mrs Goodge snatched up the menus and stuffed them in her apron. 'And something to eat as well.'

Within moments, Wiggins had appeared and the entire household gathered around the table to have tea with the constable. They looked expectantly at the housekeeper. No one wanted to be the first to speak. They'd leave that up to Mrs Jeffries. The wrong question, the wrong attitude could have terrible consequences. Constable Griffiths wasn't stupid. If they didn't handle this just right, he could easily guess it was the household helping to investigate the inspector's cases that gave the man such success. None of them were prepared to do anything that would injure their employer. He'd been far too good to all of them.

With a barely perceptible nod of her head, Mrs Jeffries acknowledged that she understood. Then she smiled at the constable, leaned back and fired her first salvo. 'I must say, Constable, I do so admire you policemen. I don't think I could start my day by doing something as dreadful as investigating a murder. I think it's terribly, terribly brave of you.' Flattery always worked.

'Oh, there's nothing to it, really. It's all part of the job,' Griffiths replied modestly. 'Mind you, a murder like this one doesn't come along every day.'

'Who got killed?' Wiggins asked eagerly. Now that Mrs Jeffries had taken the lead, the rest of them instinctively understood how to play their own parts. Wiggins, because he was young, could get away with asking blunt, straightforward questions.

'Now that's a right interestin' question,' Griffiths replied. 'We don't know. The woman didn't have anything on her to make an identification.'

'It's a woman, then,' Mrs Goodge commented brusquely.

'Oh, how sad,' Betsy cried. Like the footman, she too stepped into her part with ease. 'Some poor woman get's murdered and they don't even know who she is. How awful . . . I'll bet she's some poor street woman down on her luck.'

'This woman weren't poor,' Griffiths said. 'She were well dressed, well fed and laying on a bench in a private garden in a posh part of town.'

'What private garden?' Smythe asked. 'Someplace near here?'

'Sheridan Square.'

'That's too close for my liking.' Mrs Goodge shook her head in disgust. 'We'll all be murdered in our beds, we will. What's the world coming to when a decent woman can't even walk the streets of London without being murdered for her money?'

'We don't think she were murdered for her money,' Griffiths said quickly. Then he blushed. 'I mean, the inspector doesn't. I overheard him talking to Constable Barnes. The garden where she were found is private. You had to have a key to get in and out. She didn't have one on her and she weren't no young woman, so we don't think she nipped over the fence. Besides, it's six foot tall and it'd be hard for even a man, let alone a middle-aged woman to get past them spikes running along the top.'

'What's that got to do with 'er bein' killed fer 'er money?' Wiggins asked. He wasn't playing a part now; he really wanted to know.

'It means whoever killed her probably had the key and let her into the garden with it,' the constable explained. 'The inspector and the others reckon she must have known her killer.'

Mrs Jeffries nodded in encouragement. 'I see. Well, I expect you gentlemen will have it all cleared up in no time.'

Stealthily, they questioned the constable until they'd wrung every little detail about the murder out of him, and then Betsy escorted him to the door.

As soon as the two of them had disappeared up the front steps, Smythe leapt to his feet. 'I think I know how we can identify the victim.'

'How?' Mrs Jeffries asked.

'She didn't fly into that garden and if she weren't layin' there last night when that Tavistock fellow took his dog out, that means she musta gone there early this mornin'. There's a hansom stand not more than a quarter of a mile from Sheridan Square. I'll nip over there and see what I can find out.'

'You think she went there by hansom cab?' Mrs Goodge asked.

'She 'ad to get there someway,' Smythe reasoned, 'and a respectable well-dressed woman walkin' the streets in the dead of night or early of a mornin' woulda been noticed by the constable on patrol. But accordin' to what Griffiths said, no one saw hide nor hair of her.'

'You're right, Smythe.' Mrs Jeffries nodded. 'There's a good chance the victim did use a cab. Go on and see what you can find out. We'll meet back here this evening.'

Smythe nodded and took off towards the back door.

'Where's he goin'?' Betsy asked as she came back to the kitchen.

'To see if the victim got to Sheridan Square by a hansom cab,' Mrs Goodge said. 'And I don't think it's fair. Smythe gets to do something, and the rest of us have to sit here twiddling our thumbs because the silly woman managed to get herself murdered without anyone knowing who she was.'

'We've plenty to do,' Mrs Jeffries said calmly. 'For starters, you've got to get that provision list ready and off to the grocer's so you can prepare to feed your sources. The larders are empty.'

'I suppose so,' Mrs Goodge agreed grudgingly. But she was still annoyed that Smythe had got the jump on them. There was just the teeniest bit of natural competition between the males and the females in the household.

'The larders really are empty,' Mrs Jeffries said again. 'If we manage to identify that woman quickly, you're going to be in a bit of a pickle if you haven't anything on hand to feed people.'

The cook decided to give in gracefully. 'You're right. I'd best be ready. Let me see, where did I put that list? Ah yes, here it is, in my pocket with the menus.'

Mrs Goodge did her investigating in her own way. She baked enough to feed an army and then opened her kitchen to dozens of London's working people. Costermongers, servants, delivery boys, rag-and-bones men, flower girls, and shoeblacks; one and all traversed through Mrs Goodge's kitchen. While they were there, she pumped them for every morsel of gossip about the suspects in a particular case. But she didn't stop there. She also had her own network of servants from other households feeding her information. She'd cooked for a number of England's finest families, and she still had connections all over the country. She was quite ruthless about using them as well.

Betsy frowned. 'It's all well and good that Mrs Goodge has something to do, but what about Wiggins and me? Are we just supposed to sit about twiddling our thumbs?'

'Of course not,' Mrs Jeffries replied. She quite understood Betsy's complaint. 'There's plenty we must do. I'd like you to nip over to Luty and Hatchet's and tell them what's happened. They'll need to be here this afternoon for our meeting.'

Luty Belle Crookshank and her butler, Hatchet, were friends of the household. They frequently helped on the inspector's cases. Luty Belle, in particular, threw a fit if she was left out.

Mollified, Betsy nodded. 'Right. Do you want me to get on over to Sheridan Square afterward and see what I can suss out?'

'Absolutely,' Mrs Jeffries agreed, 'but do be careful. You mustn't let the inspector or anyone who might recognize you catch even so much as a glimpse of you.'

'I'll be careful,' Betsy promised.

'What am I goin' to do, then?' Wiggins asked eagerly.

'You're going to get over to Sheridan Square as well,' she replied. 'But unlike Betsy, you're to make yourself known as a member of the inspector's household.'

'What?' Wiggins jaw dropped. 'Are you 'aving me on, Mrs Jeffries?'

'No,' Mrs Jeffries said bluntly. A plan was rapidly forming in her mind. 'I'm not having you on, so to speak. But I do have an idea. We need to know the identity of our victim as soon as possible. I'm going to have Mrs Goodge make up a parcel of food for you to take to our inspector. But you're not to give it to him. You're to hang on to it and use it as your excuse to poke about and see what's going on.'

By the puzzled frown on the lad's face, she could see he didn't quite get what she was trying to tell him. 'What I mean is that you're to make sure you don't make contact with our inspector until the last possible moment . . . but having the food with you will give you an excuse to be hanging about listening and, if you're very clever, asking a few questions. If anyone asks what you're doing there, you can say you're bringing the inspector something to eat.'

'Now I get it,' he bobbed his head eagerly. 'I'm to hang about and learn what I can and use the food parcel as my reason for bein' there.'

'Correct.'

'Give me a minute and I'll have the food ready,' Mrs Goodge said as she bustled toward the pantry.

'There's some buns and cheese I can put in as well as a few plums.'

'What are you going to be doing?' Betsy asked as she slipped her hat off the coat tree. 'Will you be out asking questions as well?'

'No, I'll be right here,' Mrs Jeffries replied firmly. 'Holding down the fort as it were.'

'Should we start here, sir?' Barnes pointed to the door of the house next to the Tavistock residence. Number six was much like its neighbor. As a matter of fact, it, along with virtually every other house in the square was almost identical. All of them had freshly painted white doors, and all of them were of the same uniform light gray color. The only difference between the Tavistock home and the one the constable pointed at was the color of the curtains. The ones in the windows of number six were a dark midnight blue.

Witherspoon nodded. 'I suppose this is as good a place as any.' He started up the pavement toward the short set of stairs leading to the front door. 'This is going to be quite tedious, Constable. We're going to have to talk to every household on the square.'

'Yes, sir,' Barnes replied glumly. 'I know.'

The door to number six was opened before they even knocked by a cheery-faced maid. 'Good morning, gentlemen,' she said chattily. 'You're the police, aren't you?'

'Good day, miss. You're quite correct, we are the police,' Witherspoon replied. 'We'd like to speak with the head of your household if we could.'

'That' d be Mr Prosper,' the maid replied, 'and he ain't here. He's in Edinburgh on business. Will Mrs Prosper do?'

'That will be fine.'

The maid nodded and ushered them inside. 'Just go on into the drawing room, sir,' she instructed, pointing to an open doorway down the hall, 'and I'll get the mistress.'

'Thank you,' the inspector replied. He blinked in surprise as he entered the drawing room.

'Blimey, sir,' Barnes muttered with a quick look over his shoulder to make sure he wasn't overheard, 'there's enough in here to open a shop.'

Settees, overstuffed chairs, ottomans, bookcases and cabinets crowded the huge room. Along the walls, portraits, hunting and pastoral scenes and boldly garish wall sconces competed for attention. Along the tops of the cabinets and bookcases there were knickknacks of porcelain and silver. Chinese vases, fringed shawls and elegantly draped midnight-blue curtains gave the room an air of oriental mystery. Witherspoon shook his head. 'You're quite right, Constable. I do believe one could easily stock a shop, and it appears that the stock would be quite expensive too. None of this looks cheap.'

The constable pointed to a pair of ceramic shepherds sitting atop a small cherry wood table in the corner. 'The missus saw just one of them in a shop window a few weeks back, wanted a pretty penny for it too.'

'I understand you want to see me?' A cool female voice said from behind them.

Witherspoon, blushing to the roots of his thinning hair, whirled about. 'I'm dreadfully sorry, madam,' he said to the tall, elegantly dressed woman standing in the doorway. 'I didn't hear you come in. We were just admiring your porcelain. It's quite lovely.'

'Thank you.' She nodded regally. She was a woman who was in her early thirties. Her hair was a light brown, her eyes blue and her face thin and fine boned. Slender and tall, she wore a morning dress of brilliant blue with white lace flounces along the neck and wrists. 'I'm Annabelle Prosper. The maid said you wished to speak with me.'

'Yes ma'am,' Witherspoon introduced himself and the constable. 'We do hate to disturb you,' he continued, 'but we're in the position that we must get statements from all the households in the square.'

'Please sit down.' She nodded toward the nearest settee while she took a seat on the one opposite. 'What is this about?'

'I'm afraid something rather unfortunate has happened in your garden,' the inspector said. 'There's been a murder.'

She started in surprise. 'A murder. In our garden? But that's absurd. It's locked.'

'Absurd as it may be,' the inspector assured her, 'it still happened. The victim was a middle-aged woman. She had nothing on her person to identify her. Is anyone from your household missing?'

'No.' Mrs Prosper shook her head. 'Everyone's here.'

'Are you quite certain about that, ma'am?' Barnes asked. 'This is a big house. Have you seen all your staff?'

34

Annabelle Prosper raised one delicately arched eyebrow. 'I'm quite sure, Constable. In my husband's absence, I preside over morning prayers. I assure you, the entire staff was present.'

'We weren't doubting your word, ma'am,' Witherspoon interjected hastily.

'Annabelle, I've heard there are some policemen here . . . Oh, goodness, it's true, then.' A short, dark-haired rather plump woman of middle years hurried into the drawing room.

'Really, Marlena, must you be so precipitous?' Annabelle shot the woman a disapproving frown.

The woman ignored her and advanced toward the two men. 'Hello, I'm Marlena McCabe, Mrs Prosper's sister-in-law.'

Witherspoon and Barnes both got to their feet. He looked pointedly at Mrs Prosper, who rather grudgingly introduced the two policemen. 'We were just having a word with Mrs Prosper,' he explained after the pleasantries had been exchanged.

'About the murder in the garden?' Marlena said eagerly.

'How did you know about that, ma'am?' Barnes asked.

She laughed. 'Really, Constable, did you think you'd be able to keep it a secret? There's police all over the square. I heard it from Maggie, our tweeny, and she got it from Colonel Bartell's scullery maid. Is it true that a woman's been stabbed and her head cut off?'

'Marlena!' Annabelle Prosper snapped. 'Must you be so . . . so . . .'

'No one got their head cut off, ma'am,' Wither-spoon said quickly. 'But we did find the body of a woman. That's why we're here. We're trying to deter-mine who she might be.'

'How exciting,' Marlena flopped down next to her sister-in-law. 'Maybe I can be of some help.'

'You don't know anything,' Mrs Prosper chided. 'Honestly, Marlena, you ought to be be ashamed of yourself. You mustn't interfere with an official police inquiry simply because you find it exciting.'

'I do too know something,' she replied, glaring at her sister-in-law. She looked at the policemen. 'Was the woman quite tall, wearing a plain hat and a blue traveling dress?'

Witherspoon and Barnes straightened to attention. 'She was,' the inspector said. 'Do you know her? Can you tell us who she is?'

'Well, no, not exactly,' she replied. 'But I can tell you when she arrived at the square. I saw her getting out of a hansom about five this morning.'

'You saw her?' Barnes prompted.

'From the front hall,' Marlena explained. 'I'd come downstairs to get a glass of water. No one was up at that hour, of course, and it was very quiet. I heard a carriage come into the square – they make a terrible racket, you see. It's the horses' hooves on those cob-blestones on the north side.'

'You're digressing, Marlena,' Mrs Prosper said. Now, she too looked interested. 'Do go on.'

'Well.' Marlena nodded importantly. 'As I said, I heard a carriage come in. Of course, I thought it might be Eldon back from Scotland . . .'

'Eldon's not due until this evening,' Mrs Prosper interrupted.

'Yes, I know that. But he does hate being away from home, and I thought he might have come back early, you see.' She paused for breath. 'As I was saying, I heard the carriage and, thinking it might be Eldon, I went to that window.' She pointed toward the end of the room facing the square, 'and had a look. But it wasn't Eldon, it was this woman. She got out of a hansom right in front of Mr Tavistock's house. Of course, that's right next door.'

'Did you see her go into the garden?' Witherspoon asked. She shook her head. 'No, I went back upstairs.'

'Did you hear anything after that? Anything at all that struck you as odd.' Witherspoon didn't wish to put words in the woman's mouth, but perhaps she'd heard a scream or a scuffle.

'I'm afraid not.' She shrugged apologetically. 'My room is on the second floor at the back of the house. I heard nothing.'

'And you're sure about the time,' Barnes pressed. 'It was five o'clock in the morning.'

'Quite sure,' Marlena McCabe said firmly. 'The clock in the hall had just struck the hour when I heard the hansom come into the square. I'm sorry I can't be more helpful.'

'You've been most helpful, indeed, ma'am,' Witherspoon said gratefully. 'At least now we know the victim was still alive at five this morning.' He got to his feet.

Barnes, flicking his notebook shut, got up as well.

37

'Do you remember if the garden gate was closed?' he asked as he tucked the book in his pocket.

Mrs McCabe's brows drew together in thought. 'I don't think, I know. Frankly, I wasn't looking at the garden. I was looking at the hansom. My attention was turned toward the Tavistock house. I've no idea if the gate was open or closed.'

'I quite understand, ma'am.' Witherspoon wished that people were more observant. But he could hardly say so. Especially as this woman was the first helpful witness they'd come across. 'As I said, you've been most helpful.'

'Thank you,' she replied. But she wasn't looking at the policemen; she was smirking at Mrs Prosper. 'Well, what do you think, Annabelle, have I been helpful or not?'

Annabelle smiled thinly. Clearly, she didn't like being shown up in front of strangers. 'As the inspector said, dear, you've been most helpful. Most helpful indeed.'

'Look, it's not as if I'm askin' ya to fly to the moon and back,' Smythe said in disgust. 'All I want is a bit of information.'

The cabbie yawned and rubbed his face. He leaned against the side of the small building that housed the hansom stand. Inside his mates were drinking tea and having a bit of a rest. 'You may as well ask me to fly to the moon. It's not as if you're wantin' to know if someone picked up a fare at Sheridan Square. You're wantin' to know who took a fare there. It coulda been from anywhere in the city, mate. It'da been a mite sight easier if it were the other way around. It woulda have to have been one of the local blokes if it were a pickup, but as it were a drop, it coulda come from anywhere.'

Smythe knew it was pointless getting irritated. The cabbie was right. As the victim had been dropped off and not picked up at the square, she could have come from anywhere around London. The two-mile rule only covered picking up passengers, not dropping them off. He sighed and shoved away from the lamppost he'd been leaning against. This had been a blooming wasted trip. He'd had sod all luck. No one knew anything. 'All right, then, thanks for yer 'elp.'

'Weren't much 'elp, mate.' The cabbie shrugged sympathetically. 'Not much I can tell ya. None of us around here took that fare.'

'What fare?' A tall, rawboned cabbie with red hair poking out of a battered bowler strolled up to the men.

'A fare to Sheridan Square.'

'Harry did,' the cabbie said slowly as he raked Smythe's plain working clothes with a practised eye. 'Why? What's it to you?'

'I'm lookin' fer someone,' Smythe replied. 'A woman.'

'Your woman?' the other cabbie asked.

'Never you mind whose woman she is,' he said. 'Let's just say that whoever can help me find out which of you drovers took a fare to Sheridan Square this morning will be in fer a pretty penny.' He'd decided that greasing their palms with silver would work far better than trying to come up with some silly story explaining why he wanted to track the woman down.

'How much?' the red haired man asked.

Smythe wasn't stupid enough to whip out his roll of bills in front of all and sundry. Nor was he going to part with cash until he had some information. 'First you tell me which one is 'arry and then we'll talk about how much.'

The cabbie eyed him suspiciously. 'How do I know you'll pay?'

'You don't,' Smythe sighed impatiently. He didn't want to stand here all day. 'Look, you take me to this 'arry feller and I'll make it worth yer while. Does that sound fair?'

The man thought about it for all of two seconds. 'Fair enough.' He turned on his heel and started off down the road, away from the cab stand. 'Come on, then. Get a move on. Harry's not goin' to be there long.'

Smythe nodded his thanks to the other cabbie and hurried after the tall redhead.

Wiggins tucked his small parcel neatly under his arm as he stood on the cobblestone road and gazed onto Sheridan Square. Opposite him was the garden where the poor lady had met her untimely death . . . to Wiggins any death not taken in a nice soft bed at the age of ninety was untimely. Wiggins bobbed to one side. He could see see the helmet of a constable on the far side of the garden. Probably a police constable guarding the entrance, he thought. He tucked the parcel of food under his arm, straightened his spine and strolled toward the action. After all, if anyone stopped him, he had a reason for being there.

He rounded the corner of the garden and saw that the gate was open. The constable on guard was a lad not much older than himself. Wiggins stood on tiptoe, trying to see through the thick bushes into the interior of the square. But all he could see were passing police helmets or the flash of a dark uniform as the lads searched the grounds.

He moved his gaze from the garden to the square itself. The houses were huge, well kept and reeking of money. Wiggins chuckled lightly. Most of the residents were too well-bred to show any interest in the police presence right under their noses, but they'd sent their servants out to pick up what gossip they could. In front of number six a tweeny energetically swept the doorstoop. Across from Wiggins, windows were being washed at another house and at a third, a footman was outside polishing the brass carriage lamps. None of them were paying more than passing attention to their tasks; they were all watching the garden.

Wiggins took a deep breath and started in the direction of the tweeny. A lad had to start somewhere and she was as good as any.

The girl didn't even hear him approaching. She was staring hard at the garden. Wiggins, thinking she might have a better view from this end of the square, stopped a few feet away from her and took a gander himself. He could see nothing but bushes and hedges. He glanced back at the girl. Her attention was still fixed on the square, the broom in her hands moving rhythmically back and forth as she brushed the same spot over and over. He headed towards her, taking care to walk heavily so that his footsteps sounded along the pavement. The girl started and whirled about.

'Sorry, miss,' he said quickly. 'I didn't mean to frighten you.'

'You didn't scare me,' she said defensively, 'you startled me, that's all.'

She was really very pretty, he thought. Beneath her conical maid's cap, her hair was a deep brown color. Her eyes were hazel and her skin was perfect. 'I didn't mean to,' he said. 'You was staring at that garden so hard you musta not 'eard me coming till I was right behind you. What's happened?' He jerked his head at the square.

'Someone's got murdered,' she replied. She turned her back on him and went back to sweeping.

Wiggins didn't think this was a particularly good sign. But the fact that he'd have to talk to her back didn't stop him. 'Murdered? Really? How?'

'I don't know,' she muttered.

He knew that was a lie. By now, he knew that every servant in the square knew how the victim had died. 'Well, I can see talkin' about it upsets you, miss,' he said sympathetically. 'So I'll not trouble you with any more questions. But could you tell me if you've seen a policeman . . .'

'I've seen half a dozen coppers,' she snapped over her shoulder. 'They're all over the garden and the square.'

'But I'm lookin' for a particular one, miss,' he continued calmly. 'An inspector. He's my guy, he is. I've got a packet of food our cook sent over for 'im.'

The girl turned and stared at him. 'You work for one of them policemen?'

'I work for the man in charge,' Wiggins bragged. 'Inspector Witherspoon. If you've 'ad a murder 'ere, 'e'll find the killer. 'E's ever so good at it, 'e is. Do you know where 'e is?'

She stared at him for a moment. 'I don't know where he's gone,' she finally said. 'He were here earlier talkin' to the mistress, but then he left.'

'Left? You mean 'e's gone back to the station?'

'How should I know?' Once again she turned her back on him and began to sweep. 'It's not for the likes of me to stick my nose into anything that don't concern me.'

'But murder concerns everyone,' Wiggins protested. Then he clamped his mouth shut. His instincts were screaming at him to keep quiet for a moment. Something was going on here, something wasn't right. He'd had dozens of conversations with servants that had been close to crimes or a crime scene, and not one of them had ever acted like this girl. She wasn't excited or curious, and that just plain wasn't right. He knew what a domestic's life was like. Anything out of the ordinary, anything that took you away from the drudgery of your work, even for a few moments, was cause for excitement.

But the girl wasn't excited.

She was angry. Wiggins chewed his lower lip as he thought about what to do next. He noticed her hands were clamped around the broom handle so tightly that her knuckles were white. Her shoulders were hunched defensively, and her expression was closed and grim.

43

'Uh, miss,' he said tentatively, 'I'm really sorry I startled you.'

'It's all right,' she muttered. 'Now get on with you. I've work to do.'

'I didn't mean to interrupt you,' he continued, racking his brain for some way of prolonging the conversation. 'I really didn't. You won't get in trouble will ya? I mean, you'll not get the sack just because I stopped and spoke to ya?'

'Not if you go away now,' she said. 'But if you hang about chatting, they'll toss me out on my ear. Now get off with you.'

'Cor blimey, you must work for a strict household.'

The girl laughed. 'You could say that. Go on, go find your inspector.'

Wiggins hesitated. He sensed he'd missed his opportunity to get any more information out of the girl, but he was loath to give up so easily. He opened his mouth to ask another silly question when the front door flew open and an older woman stuck her head out. 'Fiona, get in here. You're not to spend all day sweeping that pavement.'

'Yes, ma'am,' she replied, 'I'm just coming.' She picked up her broom and disappeared around the side of the house.

Wiggins watched her leave and promised himself he'd come back later. He glanced at the house number and made a mental note that it was number six. It wouldn't do to forget where the girl lived. That Fiona knew something. He'd bet his next meal on it.

★ ★ ★

Timothy Heckston sat behind his huge rosewood desk and tapped his fingers impatiently on the desk pad. He was of late middle age but still had a head of thick blond hair, a sharp-pointed chin, thin lips and prominent cheekbones. 'I'm sorry to be so unhelpful, gentlemen,' he said with a shrug. 'But there's little else I can tell you.'

'Are you absolutely certain there are only seven keys to the garden, sir?' Inspector Witherspoon asked.

'Eight, Inspector,' Heckston corrected. 'Eight keys. Each house on the square is issued one, and the gardener has one as well.'

'Yes, of course, Mr Tavistock told us that.' Witherspoon nodded.

'Are you still in possession of Mrs Baldridge's key, sir?' Barnes asked. 'I believe she, uh, gave it back to you.'

Heckston broke into a grin. 'Heard about that, did you? She didn't give it to me, sir. She threw it at my head.'

Barnes smiled. 'We understand Mrs Baldridge is a great lover of hollyhocks.'

'Silly woman couldn't understand that the wretched things wouldn't grow in the garden.' He stood up, walked across the room to a small cupboard next to the door. Taking a small key out of his pocket, he unlocked the cupboard and opened it. 'You'd have thought we were deliberately trying to upset her. I was as gentle as possible . . .' he stopped and a frown crossed his face. 'That's odd. It's not here.'

Witherspoon glanced at Barnes and then said, 'What's not there, sir?'

'The key.' Heckston turned and stared at them, his expression puzzled. 'Mrs Baldridge's key isn't there. It's gone.'

'Are you sure, sir?' Barnes asked. He and the inspector had both risen to their feet. They crossed the room and stood behind Heckston's shoulder. The cupboard was lined with three rows of hooks. The top two rows had keys of various sizes hanging from them with small, white labels affixed beneath them. The bottom row, the row labeled 'Garden Keys' was completely empty.

Heckston pointed to the last hook on that row. 'Mrs Baldridge's key was right here.'

'Could it have been misplaced, sir?' Barnes asked.

Heckston shook his head. 'No one opens this cupboard but me, sir. I always keep it locked.'

'What about other members of your household?' Witherspoon prodded.

'Other than myself, there's only my wife who has a key. She'd have no reason to bother with garden keys.'

'When was the last time you saw the key, sir?' the inspector asked quickly. He'd found that if one kept up a steady stream of questions, one sometimes found that the person one was questioning didn't have time to make up any lies.

'The last time.' Heckston frowned. 'Let's see. I suppose it must have been last week. Yes, yes, that's right. I opened up the cupboard to get the key to the wine cellar.'

'Was it possible the key fell out or was accidentally taken?' Barnes pressed.

'No, as you can see, the hooks are rounded so that keys can't be knocked off accidentally.'

'Was anyone else in the room with you?' Witherspoon asked. 'I mean, did anyone else know where the key was kept?'

Heckston hesitated. 'Well, I suppose so. I opened the cupboard in front of the whole garden committee. We were having a meeting, you see. We always meet in the study. It keeps things more businesslike, moves the whole process along a bit faster, if you know what I mean. Long meetings are so tiresome.'

'So you're saying, sir,' Barnes said quietly, 'that everyone on the square knew where the spare key was kept?'

Heckston nodded glumly. 'I'm afraid so.'

'Which means that anyone could have taken the key. No offense meant, Mr Heckston, but that lock doesn't look to be very sturdy.' Witherspoon said. Drat. This wasn't going to be an easy one to solve.

CHAPTER THREE

The household gathered back at Upper Edmonton Gardens at four that afternoon. Everyone was there, even Luty Belle Crookshank and her butler Hatchet. Luty Belle was an elderly, wealthy, rather eccentric American. White haired and dark eyed, she had a penchant for brightly colored clothes and an acerbic tongue that masked a heart as big as her native country. Hatchet, her butler, was tall, dignified and constantly trying to force his mistress to watch her manners.

'Really, madam.' Hatchet sniffed as they took their places at the table. 'You might have managed to be a bit kinder to Countess Rutherford. I don't believe she much appreciated being told she had to leave because you had something important to do.'

'Then she ought to have taken the hint,' Luty shot back quickly. 'I'd spent ten minutes droppin' little niceties to git the woman outa my drawin' room. But she didn't budge. I don't like being mean to people, but Nell's bells, that woman could talk a grizzly into a cave. I didn't think I'd ever git rid of her.'

Mrs Jeffries smiled at the two of them. She knew perfectly well that Hatchet was speaking more out of habit than anything else. She was sure that if Luty hadn't gotten rid of Countess Rutherford, he would have. He wouldn't let anyone, titled or not, stand in the way of a murder investigation. Both of them enjoyed snooping far more than entertaining. After Luty had inadvertently gotten involved in one of the household's first cases, she'd come to them for help to find a missing girl. After that, it would have been difficult to keep either her or Hatchet out of their investigations.

'I'm sorry you had to get rid of your guest,' the housekeeper said apologetically, 'but I thought you'd want to be here. Even though at this point we don't know all that much.'

'You thought right,' Luty said. 'What have we got? Betsy's message this mornin' weren't real detailed.'

'Sorry about that,' Betsy smiled. 'I know I should have stayed and told you everything, but I was in a hurry to get out and about.'

'Don't concern yourself, Miss Betsy,' Hatchet said. 'Your message was fine. Unlike Madam, I realized immediately that you'd not learned more than the bare facts of the case.'

'Speakin' of which,' Luty said, 'maybe you could rest yer tongue a minute so Hepzibah can share those details with us.' She was the only one to ever call the housekeeper by her Christian name.

Mrs Jeffries quickly said, 'We still don't know who the victim was.' She told them about the woman being found in the locked garden and about how the victim had been stabbed.

'A locked garden?' Puzzled, Luty shook her head. 'Why go to so much trouble? Nell's bells, there's half a dozen places to stab someone in the middle of the night.'

'I agree,' Mrs Jeffries replied. 'I've spent a good part of today thinking the same thing. The circumstances of the murder are very, very strange.'

'Not if the killer planned on meetin' the victim in that garden,' Wiggins said. 'I've seen the place. It's a right good place for murder. The bushes and such is so high you can do what you like and not be seen from the street.'

'But she was killed in the middle of the night,' Betsy said. 'You don't need bushes for that. All you need is darkness. I agree with Luty and Mrs Jeffries. Luring someone into a garden in the dead of night is a strange way to commit murder. Why go to all that bother? Why not just meet them on a deserted public street and wait till their back is turned?'

'It's hardly convenient,' Mrs Jeffries said. 'Especially as we know that the killer had to have had a key.'

'Or the victim had one,' Hatchet said thoughtfully. 'And the killer took it with him when he left.'

Mrs Jeffries knew that too much speculation at this point might be dangerous. On more than one of their past investigations, they'd done their snooping with a whole set of preconceived notions that had turned out to be just plain wrong. She didn't want that to happen here. 'Well, let's keep an open mind, shall we? I do hope that one of you has learned something useful today? Otherwise we'll have to wait until the inspector comes home, and that might not be till quite late.'

'I think I might know a few things,' Wiggins volunteered eagerly. ''Angin' about was a right good idea, I overheard 'alf a dozen coppers talkin'.'

'Excellent, Wiggins.' Mrs Jeffries beamed proudly at the lad. 'Do tell us everything.'

Wiggins took a fast sip of his tea. 'For starters, I overheard one of the coppers sayin' that the inspector 'ad found a witness who'd seen the victim arrivin' in the square.'

'That's a good start,' Luty encouraged. 'What time did she git there?'

'It weren't the middle of the night. It were five in the mornin',' he continued, 'and she come by hansom.'

'Who's the witness?' Smythe asked softly.

'A lady who lives at number six, her name's McCabe. Mrs McCabe.' Wiggins frowned. 'Why do ya want to know? Don't you believe me?'

'Of course I do, ya silly git,' Smythe said. 'As a matter of fact, I found the driver that brung the woman there. I just thought it might be important to know who else was up and about at five in the mornin', that's all.' He turned his attention to the housekeeper. 'To tell ya the truth, Mrs J, we're in a bit of a pickle. Ya see, I didn't just find the hansom driver. I think I found out who the victim was. I can't for the life of me think of a way to let the inspector know.'

'You know who she is?' Luty exclaimed. 'Hell's fire and apple butter, that'll put us way ahead of the police.'

'Excellent work, Smythe,' Hatchet said proudly. 'We really are good, aren't we?'

'Goodness, you're ever so clever, Smythe.' Betsy

smiled at him and patted his arm. 'I wish I'd been able to find out who she was.'

'Good work,' Mrs Goodge said. 'Knowing who our victim is will save us a lot of time and trouble.'

'Gracious, Smythe,' Mrs Jeffries said, 'you've managed quite a feat. Who was she?'

'That's just it.' Smythe shook his head. 'She weren't nobody. I mean, she were somebody, but she couldn't be somebody anyone would want to kill. Not unless-in' they was a lunatic like that ripper feller. Ya see, the woman couldn't have had any enemies in England. She'd just arrived here the day before from Australia. Why would anyone want to kill a perfect stranger?'

'We're not doing all that well, are we, sir?' Barnes asked glumly as they made their way to the last house on the square. 'Mrs Lucas at number two was sound asleep, and so were her servants. What do you think of Colonel Bartell, sir? Do you think he was telling the truth?'

'About being awake but hearing nothing.' Witherspoon smiled sadly. 'Oh, yes, I'm quite sure he was telling the truth. I don't think his hearing is all that good. If you'll recall, he kept his head cocked toward us the whole time we were there. As for him being awake, I imagine that's true too. Many elderly people have difficulty sleeping through the night. It's too bad there aren't more people like that helpful Mrs McCabe at number six. She, at least, saw something useful.'

'Most people aren't up at five, sir,' Barnes said with a frown. 'I'll tell you the truth, sir, I'm not looking forward to this one.' He jerked his chin toward the house they were rapidly approaching. 'Mrs Baldridge sounds like she's got a bit of a temper.'

Witherspoon hadn't been looking forward to it either; that's why he'd left it to last. 'Let's hope she'll be more cooperative with the police than she was with the garden committee.' He sighed as they reached the Baldridge house. He couldn't put this off any longer, he thought, as he started up the short flight of steps.

The front door flew open, and a round-faced, smiling girl with a maid's cap on stuck her head out. 'You must be the police,' she said cheerfully. She pulled the door open wide and gestured for them to come inside. 'Do come in, sirs. The mistress has already ordered tea. We've been waiting for you. She wondered what was taking you so long.'

Bemused, Witherspoon glanced at Barnes. The constable looked as puzzled as the inspector. They followed the maid down a long hallway, their footsteps echoing loudly on the polished oak floor. From what the inspector had heard of Mrs Baldridge, he certainly wouldn't have thought she'd be in any hurry to speak with the police. So few people were.

The girl lead them through a set of double oak doors and into a large, elegant drawing room. There were cream-colored damask curtains at the windows, a lovely Persian carpet and several comfortable-looking settees and love seats arranged imaginatively about the room. On the settee farthest from the door sat a well-dressed woman. A silver tea service was spread out on a low table in front of her. She stared at the two men curiously as they approached. Middle-aged and with fading brown hair pulled up in a topknot, she had dark, rather intelligent-looking brown eyes, a full mouth and a long, straight nose.

The inspector was rather surprised. Though well past her first youth, she was rather an attractive, pleasant-looking person. Not the kind of woman one would imagine hurling a set of keys at someone. He really didn't know what to make of this. 'Good day, madam. I'm Inspector Gerald Witherspoon and this is Constable Barnes.'

'I know who you are, Inspector,' she replied. A hint of a smile crossed her face. 'I've been waiting for you. Please sit down and make yourselves comfortable. As you can see, I've taken the liberty of ordering tea. I do hope you and your constable will have it with me.'

'Thank you, ma'am,' Witherspoon said gratefully. His mouth watered. He tried not to stare at the food, but he'd not had much to eat since breakfast. Temptingly spread out on the table before him were trays of sandwiches, scones, Madeira cake and sliced buttered bread. 'That's very kind of you.'

'Do help yourselves to something to eat,' she said matter-of-factly as she poured the tea. 'I'm sure you're both hungry. You've been out on the square for hours. I don't quite see how you do it. All that investigating on an empty stomach.'

'Actually, my footman brought us a spot of lunch,' the inspector said as he helped himself to a slice of thick brown bread. But as he'd shared most of it with Barnes and two uniformed lads, they'd not had enough to fill them up.

'Most of which you shared with me and the other lads,' Barnes put in.

'Then I'm sure you're both quite hungry. Please, do help yourselves,' she ordered briskly. She handed each man his tea and then picked up her own pink and white porcelain cup. 'I expect you want to ask me a few questions, don't you?'

Witherspoon finished loading a scone on his plate before answering. 'Did you hear or see anything early this morning? By that, I mean, did you hear or see anything out of the ordinary? Anything that struck you as odd.'

'Of course I did, Inspector.' She smiled. 'That's why I wanted to speak with you.'

'How very fortunate for us,' he replied. Perhaps this time he'd be very lucky on a case, and there would actually be a useful witness to the murder. He slapped a piece of buttered bread next to the scone. 'What did you see, ma'am?'

'I didn't see anything.'

'I beg your pardon?' He put his plate down and gave her his full attention.

She raised an eyebrow. 'I didn't see anything, sir. I heard something.'

'What would that be ma'am?' Barnes asked. He too put his plate down and whipped out his little brown notebook.

'Before I give you the details,' she said thoughtfully, 'there's something you need to understand. Since my husband passed away, I've had a great deal of trouble sleeping. Consequently, I find myself wide awake at the most ridiculous hours.'

'Was that the case last night?' the inspector asked.

'Very much so,' she sighed. 'I awoke at half past

55

four this morning. I know exactly what time it was because I got up and looked at the clock. Well, of course one can't wake their servants up at such an awful hour, so I put on my robe and decided to go downstairs for a cup of tea. I was just coming down the front stairs when I heard someone outside in the street.'

'Heard someone?' Witherspoon frowned. 'Precisely how? Did you hear a hansom?'

'I heard footsteps,' she said. 'It's extraordinary how quiet it is at that hour of the morning.'

'Yes, ma'am,' Witherspoon agreed slowly. 'Er . . . uh, it is very quiet at that time of the morning.'

'You don't understand,' she said impatiently. 'I didn't make that comment as an idle observation, Inspector. I made it because it is quite pertinent to your case.'

'Pertinent,' Witherspoon echoed. 'Yes, yes, I'm sure it is.' He was rather puzzled. 'But are you positive it was half past four when you heard these footsteps?'

'The very latest it could have been was four thirty-five,' she said firmly. 'It doesn't take long to don a robe and come down one flight of stairs.'

'I'm sure it doesn't,' he replied quickly. 'I'm not disputing your word, ma'am. I'm merely making certain I understand you completely.'

'You're not asking the right questions, sir,' she admonished. 'Aren't you at all curious as to why I think those footsteps are pertinent?'

'I was just getting ready to ask that,' he said.

'Good, because if you must know, I'm quite sure the footsteps must have been those of the killer.' She leaned forward eagerly. 'You see, the reason I made the remark about the quiet is because whoever was walking by the front door took care to be as quiet as possible. But they couldn't mask their footsteps completely, and I heard them.'

Witherspoon thought he understood what she was saying. 'You mean you think they were taking care not to make any noise.'

'Whoever it was out there was creeping about on his tiptoes,' she said.

'How can you be sure of that, ma'am?' Barnes asked curiously.

'Because I don't sleep much,' she said bluntly. 'And I've heard all manner of people go by outside at night. Whoever was out there early this morning was deliberately trying to be quiet. And not because they were being considerate of their neighbors, either, but because they had murder in their hearts. Believe me, I know what I'm talking about. There's plenty of people around here who don't give a toss for whether or not they're disturbing their neighbors.'

The inspector wasn't quite sure how to take this sort of evidence. He didn't wish to offend the lady, but he couldn't quite see how she could be so sure about the sound of footsteps. Still, his 'inner voice,' the one that Mrs Jeffries always assured him would keep him on track, was telling him not to discount this lightly.

His consternation must have shown on his face because Mrs Baldridge suddenly sighed. 'Inspector, I can imagine what you've heard about me. But I assure you, I'm neither an hysteric nor a shrew.'

'Really, ma'am,' Witherspoon blustered. 'Such a thought never crossed my mind.'

'Let us be frank, Inspector.' She waved her hand dismissively. 'I'm sure you've heard all about the garden key incident. But I only tossed it at Mr Heckston because he was making such a fool of himself.'

'Not because of the hollyhocks?' Barnes asked.

'Certainly not.' She grinned broadly. 'I don't care what kind of flowers they plant in that stupid garden. I was only fed up because Mrs Prosper snidely remarked they were "common" when I suggested them. Well, really. Who on earth did she think she was fooling? The woman was nothing more than a lady's maid before she married Eldon Prosper, and of course that love-struck fool Heckston agreed with her.'

'Her name was Mirabelle Daws,' Smythe said softly, 'and this was her first visit to England. She come in on the *Island Star*, and that only come into port late yesterday afternoon.'

'Which port?' Hatchet asked quickly.

'Southampton,' Smythe replied. 'Miss Daws took the last train up last night. It was supposed to arrive at the station at midnight, but there was some trouble on the line and it didn't get in till half past three. That was where the cabbie picked her up. He didn't want to take her all the way over to Sheridan Square, but she offered to pay him double, being as it was in the middle of the night.'

'Gracious, you've learned far more than we'd hoped,' Mrs Jeffries said.

Smythe grinned. 'The cabbie were a bit of a talker

but more importantly, so was Miss Daws. Seems she told him what she thought of British trains, British ships and British weather before she even got into the hansom. Didn't like us much, that was fer certain. But that's 'ow come he came to know the name of the ship and all. She was goin' on a mile a minute about the ship being late, the train bein' late and the air smellin' to 'igh 'eaven.' He suddenly sobered. 'I know we've learned a lot. Now I want to know 'ow we're goin' to get this information to the inspector. It's not like you can drop a few 'ints and 'ave 'im suss out what you're goin' on about.'

'I know,' Mrs Jeffries murmured thoughtfully. 'We do seem to have a problem. But we'll think of something; we always do. In the meantime, there's no time to lose.' She hesitated for a brief moment. 'I know it's late, but do you think you can take the carriage and get to Southampton tonight? I think it's imperative that we find out who else might have been on that ship with Mirabelle Daws.'

'That's not goin' to be easy,' Luty put in. 'The ship come in yesterday. Most people don't hang around that long. They git on about their business and go home.'

'But the crew's still there,' Hatchet said gleefully. 'Surely there's a porter or a steward who'll be able to help us.' He rose to his feet. 'If it's all right with madam, I'd like to accompany Smythe. The two of us can cover far more territory together than apart.'

Luty snorted derisively. 'Since when have you ever asked my permission to do anything? But I'd like to go with ya . . .' her voice trailed off as everyone at the table protested at the same time. She glared at all of them. 'You all think I'm too old to be gallavantin' out at night having adventures, do ya?'

'No, Luty, of course not,' Mrs Jeffries said soothingly. But, of course, that's precisely what they thought. 'We simply think you'd better stay here and help the rest of us come up with a plausible way to get the information we received to the inspector. You've a much better imagination than I have. All I can come up with is the same silly old idea I always have, an anonymous note.'

Luty eyed the housekeeper suspicously for a few moments. 'You sure you ain't just sayin' that cause you think I'm too old?'

'We're all gettin' old,' Mrs Goodge interrupted. 'But that's not why we want you to stay. Like Mrs Jeffries says, we've got some hard thinkin' to do, and your mind is sharp as one of my best kitchen knives. Now sit down, drink your tea and let's get these men out of here so we women can have a good think on how to get us out of this mess. And don't think it's not a right old mess, because it is. We're honor bound to give the inspector the woman's name, but I, for one, don't want him gettin' any more suspicious about us than he already is.'

'Does that mean I ought to go too?' Wiggins asked eagerly. 'I'm one of the men. With the three of us, we could cover even more territory.'

'I reckon I ought to stay then.' Luty leaned back in her chair. 'I do have an idea or two about how we can let the inspector know who the woman was. Like Mrs Goodge says, we don't want him gettin' any ideas about us. No offense meant, Hepzibah, but you're right, that anonymous note trick is wearin' thin.'

They'd used it several times before in their investigations, so Mrs Jeffries could hardly take offense.

Smythe rose to his feet. 'Which carriage should we take? Ours or Luty's?'

'Take mine,' Luty said quickly. 'I can always get a hansom home. That'll save you havin' to go over to Howards and gettin' your own livery out.'

'Can I go too?' Wiggins asked again as he got up. 'I really think I ought to; I am one of the men.' Fred, seeing his beloved Wiggins move, uncurled himself from his comfortable spot on the rug and trotted over to the footman.

'How are they going to find out anything?' Betsy asked. 'By the time they get down there, it'll be late at night.'

'Don't worry about that, Miss Betsy,' Hatchet said cheerfully. 'It'll not take all that long to reach our destination. There's a train at six for Southampton and once we're there, I've an idea finding out which pub the ships crew hangs about is going to be easy.'

'But I thought we was goin' to take the carriage,' Wiggins said.

Hatchet shook his head. 'We'll take the carriage to the station. The train's much faster than even the madam's fine team of horses.'

'What if the ship has already sailed?' Luty asked. 'What then?'

'She won't have sailed,' Smythe said confidently. 'I've taken ships between here and Australia. They always need at least two days portside to take on provisions and make repairs. It's a hard trip.'

Betsy's eyes narrowed. 'Exactly how many times have you done it, then?' He'd only mentioned one trip to Australia.

'Three, maybe four times,' he answered honestly, thinking she was doubting his knowledge of the ships' port time. It was only when he saw her jaw drop that he realized what he'd just let slip. 'I've told you about my trips to Australia,' he said. He had a horrible feeling in the pit of his stomach.

'You most certainly have not,' she shot back, 'and considerin' how much we talk, I'm surprised all your world traveling hasn't come up in the conversation.'

Smythe could have kicked himself for being so stupid. He'd not mentioned the last couple of trips to Australia because he'd not wanted to tell her the reason he'd made them. Mainly, to check on his rather substantial holdings in that country.

'They really ought to get going right away,' Mrs Jeffries interjected. She could tell by the expression on Betsy's face that a real storm was in the making. But the lass would just have to hold her peace until she and the coachman could be alone together. Besides, Mrs Jeffries rather suspected she knew the reason Smythe hadn't mentioned his other trips to Australia.

'Do I get to go?' Wiggins asked for the third time. 'And Fred too?'

'You can come, but not the dog,' Smythe said as he edged toward the back door. 'The inspector will want to know where he is when he comes home. You know he likes to take him for a walk before he goes to bed.' He was watching Betsy as he made his way across the room. Cor blimey, the lass was boiling. Maybe when he had a moment or two, he'd tell her the truth. But just as quickly, he decided maybe he wouldn't. He loved Betsy too much to risk losing her over the lie he was living.

'You will be careful going home, madam,' Hatchet said as he trotted after Smythe. Wiggins was right on his heels.

'You worry about yerself, Hatchet,' she snapped. 'I may be old, but I can still take care of myself.'

'I don't doubt it for a moment, madam.'

'Stay, Fred,' Wiggins told the dog. 'Smythe's right, the inspector will want to take you walkies when he gets home.'

'I'm not sure what time we'll be back,' Smythe said. 'But don't wait up for us.' With that, they disappeared down the hall.

'We won't,' Betsy yelled. She turned to the house-keeper. 'Who does he think he is? Even if they take the ruddy train, they'll not be back until tomorrow. What are we going to tell the inspector?'

'We'll tell him that Smythe took the horses for a good, long run and that he took Wiggins with him.' Mrs Jeffries was fairly sure Inspector Witherspoon wouldn't notice his footman and coachman were gone. Not when he was in the middle of murder investigation. 'Now, I think we'd better put our heads together and decide how we can tell him who the victim was.'

'I know what we should do,' Luty stated. She picked

up her teacup and took a dainty sip. 'And I must say, I think it's right imaginative.'

'Are you goin' to tell us, then?' Mrs Goodge demanded. She was a bit put out that the victim was such a nobody, and a foreign nobody at that. She'd be hard put to contribute much to this investigation.

'Course I'm goin' to tell ya. We're in this together, ain't we?' She took another sip of tea. 'I know exactly how we'll tell the inspector.'

'How?' Betsy demanded. She was in a bit of testy mood herself.

'We'll send him a telegram.'

'A telegram?' Mrs Jeffries said with a puzzled frown. 'I'm afraid I don't see how that would be all that different than sending him an anonymous note.'

'Sure it would,' Luty stated flatly. 'Cause this won't be anonymous. We'll sign it. We just won't use our own names.'

'I must say, the house is very quiet this evening,' Witherspoon said as he picked up the glass of sherry his housekeeper had so thoughtfully had poured and waiting for him when he arrived home.

'That it is, sir. There's only you, me and Mrs Goodge here. We weren't sure what your schedule might be, sir,' she said. She gave an embarrassed shrug. 'I'm afraid that Smythe and Wiggins had planned on taking the horses out for a long run and, well, they weren't sure whether or not you'd need them, so they went ahead with their plans. I do hope you don't mind, sir. I don't expect them back until late tonight.'

'They didn't take Fred, did they?' Witherspoon

asked quickly. He did look forward to his nightly walk with the dog. Especially as he and Lady Cannonberry generally used that time to have a few moments alone together.

'Of course not, sir.' Mrs Jeffries smiled. 'Fred would be very put out if he missed his evening walkies, sir. You know how devoted the animal is to you.'

'Oh, Fred likes everyone.' He frowned suddenly. 'Uh, where is Betsy? She didn't go with them, did she? I know that she and Smythe seem to have some sort of an understanding, but I don't think we ought to . . . uh . you know . . . uh . . .'

'Betsy has accompanied Luty Belle home in a hansom cab. She'll be back shortly, sir.'

Witherspoon blushed. 'Er, I didn't mean to imply anything untoward about Betsy and Smythe. It's just that I feel responsible for the girl . . . not that Smythe would ever do anything dishonorable . . . oh dear, I'm not very good at this sort of thing, am I?'

Mrs Jeffries knew precisely what he meant. 'On the contrary, sir. You're excellent at it, sir.'

'You're most kind, Mrs Jeffries,' he sighed. 'I must admit, I do wish that Smythe would get on with it. I think we could all sleep a good deal better if he'd just make his intentions clear to us all. I'm sure he wants to marry Betsy.'

'I'm sure he will marry her,' she replied. 'Eventually. But I don't think that either of them is in any hurry.' She really didn't want to discuss Smythe and Betsy's courtship. She wanted to talk about the murder. 'How did your investigation go today, sir? Was it dreadful?'

'Oh, not as awful as it could have been.' He made a face and took another quick sip of sherry. 'The poor woman had been stabbed in the back. But it wasn't as messy as some I've seen.'

'Do you have any idea of why she was killed?'

'None at all.'

'Were there any witnesses, sir?'

'Not really,' he sighed again. 'Though we do have two people who heard some unusual activity last night. I say, Mrs Jeffries, it's the oddest thing. I don't quite know what to make of it.'

'Oh, do tell me, sir,' she pleaded with a smile. 'You know how interested I am in your cases.'

He smiled happily. It was always such a relief to talk his cases out. It always gave him a new perspective on the crime. 'Let's see, where should I begin?'

'Why don't you tell me what you thought was so odd, sir?' she suggested. 'I'm terribly curious.'

'Good idea.' He reached for his glass again. 'You know the victim was found in Sheridan Square. That's quite a nice area. Rather expensive and large houses. There's only seven residences around the square, and what was odd was that we had someone from a house at each end of the square hear something early this morning.'

'What did they hear, sir?'

'Mrs Baldridge – she lives at number one, that's at one end of the square – claims she heard someone creeping by her windows early in the morning. Yet we've evidence from Mrs McCabe, who lives at the other end of the square, that she heard a hansom come into the square a good half hour after

Mrs Baldridge swears she heard footsteps. It's most mystifying.'

Mrs Jeffries didn't find it in the least mystifying. 'How so, sir?'

'I'm not sure,' he muttered, 'it just is. I mean, was it the killer creeping about at half past four, or was it the victim?'

'I should think it was the killer,' Mrs Jeffries said firmly. 'Why would the victim try to be quiet? By the way, have you any idea who the poor woman might be?'

'No,' he sighed again. 'We haven't a clue. I tell you, it's all very, very, confusing.'

'It's always confusing in the beginning, sir,' she said stoutly. 'But you know how very, very good you are at solving murders, sir. You'll catch the killer in the end. You always do.'

'It's reassuring that you have such faith in my abilities,' he said softy. 'But sometimes I doubt myself.'

'Nonsense, sir. You should never doubt yourself.'

'Thank you, Mrs Jeffries.' He smiled. 'I must admit, it does help to talk about it. You know, the people on that square were a tad uncooperative. You'd think they'd do everything they could to help us solve this case, especially as it was right on their own doorstep, so to speak.'

'Indeed, you would, sir,' she agreed.

He continued talking about the murder. Mrs Jeffries occasionally clucked her tongue or asked a question. By the time he'd finished his sherry, he'd told her every little detail about the crime.

'You must have had quite a day, sir,' she commented,

when it was apparent he'd told her everything he knew. 'I expect you'd like your dinner now.'

'Oh yes, I am a bit hungry.' He got up and started for the dining room. 'What's Mrs Goodge laid on for us this evening?'

'Lancashire hot pot, sir.' She followed him out into the hall, 'and there's lemon tarts for dessert, sir.'

They were almost at the dining room when there was a loud knock on the front door. Mrs Jeffries turned and started in that direction.

'No, Mrs Jeffries.' Witherspoon gently pulled her back. 'This time of night I don't want you or Betsy answering the door.'

'It's not that late, sir,' she protested.

'Nevertheless, I'd feel better if you let me get it.' With that, he marched down the hall and threw open the front door.

'Telegram for Inspector Witherspoon, sir,' a young lad in a messenger's uniform said.

'I'm Inspector Witherspoon.' He reached for the pale brown envelope the boy held out. 'Thank you,' he said as he took the telegram in one hand and reached in his trouser pocket with the other. Withdrawing a coin, he handed it to the lad. 'For your trouble.'

'Thank you, sir,' the boy said as he pocketed the money.

Witherspoon closed the door and stared at the envelope as though he'd never seen one before.

'Aren't you going to open it, sir?' Mrs Jeffries asked.

'Oh, yes, I suppose I ought to.' The inspector grinned sheepishly and tore it open. Taking out the slender, thin yellow paper, he read it quickly. His eyebrows rose, and Mrs Jeffries noticed he read the page again. 'Good gracious,' he exclaimed. 'This is most extraordinary. Most extraordinary, indeed.'

'What is it, sir?'

'Let me read it to you. "Dear Inspector",' he read, '"The woman who was stabbed in Sheridan Square is one Miss Mirabelle Daws. She arrived from Australia yesterday evening on a ship called the *Island Star.*"'

'Goodness, sir, that is extraordinary.' Mrs Jeffries wondered if it were Betsy's or Luty's idea to provide the name of the vessel. She wasn't sure they ought to have given so much away, but it wasn't her plan. 'Who is it from?'

'That's extraordinary as well.' He shook his head. 'I've no idea.'

'You mean it's unsigned?'

'It's signed; it's just I've never heard of this person.' He shook his head and glanced back at the message. 'It's signed, "Your humble servant, Rollo Puffy."'

'And you've no idea who he is?' she asked. Really, where did Luty come up with these strange names?

'I've no idea. No idea at all.'

'You're certain, sir?' She pressed. She wanted to make sure there wasn't a real Rollo Puffy out and about somewhere in London. Occasionally, Luty's sense of humor overcame her good sense.

'Absolutely, Mrs Jeffries,' he insisted. 'I don't think I'd ever forget meeting someone with a name like that.'

CHAPTER FOUR

The next morning, Betsy was still furious, She ignored the admiring glances of the young lad sweeping the sidewalk in front of the fishmonger and charged toward her destination, a grocer on the far corner. She wasn't on Sheridan Square, but the nearest shopping street to it. She was determined to have something useful to tell the others this afternoon.

When Smythe – she kicked a small pebble out of her way – finally took it into his head to come home today, she wanted to make damned sure she had something better to report than he did.

She dodged around a fruit-loaded hand cart blocking the pavement in front of a greengrocer and kept on walking. She might as well see what the shopkeepers had to say. At least now she had a name.

It wasn't simply rivalry that had prompted her to leave the house so early this morning in search of clues. Yesterday she'd been deeply, deeply hurt. She'd been so sure she and Smythe were coming to an understanding, had truly gotten to know each other. She'd told him things about herself she'd never shared with anyone, and he, the ruddy sod, hadn't bothered to tell her a blooming thing. Though that wasn't quite true, she was in no mood to be fair.

Luckily, by the time she arrived at the grocer's, she'd walked some of her anger off. Pulling open the door, she stepped inside. As it was just past opening, she was the only customer in the place.

'Can I help you, miss?' a thin-faced young man said from behind the counter.

'Yes, thank you.' Betsy gave him her most dazzling smile. 'I'd like a tin of Bird's Custard Powder, Epps Cocoa and some Adam's Furniture Polish, if you have it.'

'We've all those things, Miss.' He blushed deeply. 'I'll get them for you.'

In a few moments, the items she'd ordered were on the counter in front of her. 'I say, isn't it awful about that poor woman they found murdered over on Sheridan Square?'

'It's dreadful, miss. Right dreadful.' He tallied up the bill on a sheet of brown paper. 'We don't often get things like that in this neighborhood. Well, you can see by the houses and such it's a very nice area.'

'I hear she was stabbed clean throught the heart,' Betsy continued. 'Poor Miss Daws, she simply didn't stand a chance, did she? Not with someone out to murder her.'

He looked up from his figures. 'Daws?' he repeated.

'Yes,' Betsy said quickly. 'I heard it was a lady named Mirabelle Daws . . .'

'I'm afraid you must be mistaken.' He shook his

71

head. 'Awful isn't it, how people simply don't get things right?'

'What do you mean?' she demanded.

'Well.' He dropped his pencil onto the countertop. 'There was a Miss Annabelle Daws in this neighborhood . . .'

'Is she dead too?'

'No, no, she's not dead, she's married. She's now Mrs Eldon Prosper. She's also alive and well, so I don't think she could be the woman who was murdered.'

Betsy stared at him so hard that he blushed again.

'I'm sorry, I didn't mean to sound so . . .'

'Don't apolgize.' She gave him that dazzling smile again. She'd struck gold. 'It's I who should be apologizing to you. I must say, you must be ever so clever to know so much about the people in your neighborhood.'

'I'm not really very clever,' he replied, 'it's really my mum. She owns this place. She'd talk the hair off a dog, she would. She doesn't mind asking the most impertinent questions. A lot of housemaids and tweenies come in here, Mum talks them half to death before they can get what they're after an' make an escape. Mind you, she doesn't mean any harm, she simply likes to know about people. That's how come I know the name *Daws*. Mum knows everything about everyone around here.'

Betsy dearly wished it was the mother standing in front of her and not the son. 'Your mum sounds a right nice person,' she said stoutly. 'There's nothing wrong with wanting to know a bit about people, is there? It's natural, isn't it? Uh, is your mum going to be here anytime soon?'

'Nah, she's gone to Cheshire to visit my gran.' He shrugged. 'She'll not be back till next week.'

'That's too bad,' she said. She clucked sympathetically. 'It must be lonely for you, all on your own.'

'Well, it is a bit,' he admitted. 'You get used to having a bit of company.'

'Maybe I ought to hang about awhile and talk to you,' she offered. 'After all, it's not like you've got much business this morning, is it?'

'I've never heard of Rollo Puffy either,' Barnes admitted. He handed the inspector back the telegram. 'But at least we've got the victim's name now. That's a good place to start.'

'If it's the right name,' the inspector replied.

'Well, sir, it's the only one we've got,' the constable pointed out. 'So we might as well ask about if anyone's heard of the woman.'

'Of course, Constable. Yet I can't help wondering if it might have been the killer who sent the message. I mean, who else could have known who the woman was? Why send a telegram? Why not, if one were innocent, simply come along to police and identify her?'

'I don't know, sir,' Barnes said. He stopped in front of Malcolm Tavistock's house. 'It's a puzzle. What did the telegraph office say? Could they remember who'd sent it?'

'Vaguely. I went along to there myself early this morning. The night clerk was just going off duty. But he remembered who sent the message. It was a street arab. A young lad came in with the money and the message already written out.'

'Would the clerk be able to identify the boy?' Even as he asked the question, the constable knew the answer. Street arabs were thick as fleas on dogs in London.

Witherspoon shook his head. 'No, boys come in all the time to send messages. The clerk doesn't even bother to look at them. He merely takes the money and sends the telegram. But perhaps now that we've a name, we'll be able to connect the woman with someone on the square.'

'Let's hope so, sir,' Barnes muttered. 'Otherwise, we might have a devil of a time trying to locate all the passengers who came in with the woman on the *Island Star*.' He knocked on Tavistock's front door and announced his business to the maid. A few minutes later, he and the inspector were sitting in Tavistock's drawing room for the second time.

Malcolm, with Hector trotting at his heels, made his appearance a few moments later. 'Good day, Inspector,' he said politely, but he looked less than pleased to see them. 'I do hope you've made some progress on the case. We'd like to be able to use our garden again. Was the gardener able to help you any with your inquiries? I must say, I never really liked the fellow, doesn't want to look you in the eye when he speaks, if you know what I mean.'

Witherspoon pursed his lips in annoyance. Only yesterday Tavistock had virtually assured them that the gardener wasn't capable of murder. Now that he'd had a night to think it over, it had suddenly become far more likely that the murder was done by someone poor like Jonathan Siler rather than one of their own. He wasn't surprised that Tavistock was trying to cast suspicion on the man. He'd seen that trick done many times in his investigations. 'Your gardener was most cooperative. Mr Siler was at home when the crime was committed. He knew nothing about it.'

'That's what he would say, isn't it?' Tavistock insisted.

'We've no reason not to believe him,' Witherspoon continued. 'Just as we've no reason not to believe you and the other residents of Sheridan Square. None of you, it seems, have any idea who the victim might have been. But he was able to confirm that there were only eight keys. His was safely in his possession.'

Tavistock looked taken aback. 'Well, really, what are you implying?'

'Nothing, sir.' The inspector didn't have a lot of time to waste. He was going to have to talk to everyone in the square and possibly the entire neighborhood. Again. 'We do have some more questions for you, sir. Have you ever heard of a woman named Mirabelle Daws?'

'Mirabelle Daws,' Tavistock repeated. 'Are you sure you don't mean Annabelle Daws? Daws was Mrs Prosper's maiden name . . .' his voice trailed off and his jaw gaped. 'Oh God, how awful. Of course, of course, Mrs Prosper has a sister named Mirabelle. She lives in Australia.'

'Are you sure, sir?' Barnes asked.

'Absolutely,' Tavistock bobbed his head furiously.

'I saw a letter from the woman a few months ago. I mean, I didn't read it, of course, I merely handed it back to Mrs Prosper. She'd dropped it in the garden.'

'How did you know who it was from?' Witherspoon asked. 'If you didn't look at it?'

'The signature on the bottom was quite visible when I handed it to Mrs Prosper. When I realized the name was so similar to her Christian name, I commented upon the matter, and she said the letter was from her sister in Sydney.'

'Exactly when was this?' Witherspoon asked. He wondered if the sister might have mentioned a forthcoming trip to England.

Tavistock's brows drew together as he concentrated. 'Let me see, I think it must have been no more than two months ago. It was in March.'

'You're certain, sir?'

'Of course I am. There were several of us in the garden that day. Mrs Prosper, Mr Heckston and myself. We chatted about how mild the weather was for March. The letter had slipped out of Mrs Prosper's pocket. I found it under the bench, the one in the center . . .' His voice trailed off when he realized what he was saying.

'The one where the victim was found stabbed?' Barnes finished.

Tavistock shook his head sadly. 'Poor woman. Not much of a welcome to England, is it?'

Barnes and Witherspoon exchanged a glance. 'Did you know that Mrs Prosper's sister was coming for a visit?'

'No, no, I didn't.'

'What do you think, sir?' Barnes asked as they started toward the Prosper house.

'I don't know what to think,' he admitted. 'Surely Miss Daws would have let her sister know that she was coming . . .'

'Inspector Witherspoon,' a voice called from behind them.

They turned to see Mr Heckston hurrying toward them. He doffed his hat politely. 'I thought you ought to know that I've found that key that had gone missing.'

'Really, where was it, sir?' Witherspoon said. In truth, he'd actually forgotten about the missing key.

'It was on the floor, Inspector.' Heckston shrugged in embarrassment. 'The maid must have knocked it off when she was dusting, and it got wedged inbetween the carpet and floorboards. She found it today when she was sweeping. I am sorry I didn't look more carefully when you were there.'

'No harm done, sir. At least we know where all the keys are now,' the inspector replied. He was actually quite pleased. Knowing that all the keys were accounted for narrowed the range of suspects. But then again, he thought, as they now knew the victim had a relationship with one of the residents here, it was already narrowed quite a bit.

'Well, I'll be off, sir.' He nodded at the two men. 'I've a lot to do today.'

'Before you leave, sir,' Witherspoon said, 'may I ask you a question?'

'Certainly.' Heckston said politely.

'Are you acquainted with Mrs Prosper, sir? I mean, are you more than neighbors?' The moment the words left his mouth, he realized he'd been very indelicate. Judging by Heckston's ominous frown, he'd found it indelicate as well. 'I am sorry,' Witherspoon amended. 'I didn't mean that quite the way it sounded. I do need to know if you're acquainted enough with Mrs Prosper to verify that she has a sister. It's quite important that we know.'

Heckston's expression changed from anger to surprise to shock as he realized the implication of the question. 'Good Lord, I do hope this doesn't mean what I think it does.' He swallowed. 'I'm well acquainted with Mr and Mrs Prosper. As is my wife. Mrs Prosper does have a sister. An older sister named Mirabelle.'

'Does that sister live in Australia?' Barnes asked. He always liked to double-check his facts.

Heckston nodded.

Witherspoon's expression was somber. 'Then I'm afraid we may have some very bad news for Mrs Prosper. Is Mr Prosper home?'

'Yes, I think so.' Heckston closed his eyes briefly, then looked sympathetically at the Prosper house. 'Poor Mrs Prosper. This will come as a dreadful shock. Absolutely dreadful. She was very fond of her sister.' He began to back away. 'Perhaps I ought to let you get on with it, sir. If you need to speak with me again, I'll be home later this afternoon.'

As soon as the man had cleared off, the inspector looked at Barnes. 'I suppose we'd better go and talk with Mrs Prosper.'

'Are you going to ask her to look at the body?' Barnes asked as they started walking.

'I'm afraid I don't have a choice,' the inspector replied. 'That may be the only way we can possibly have the woman identified.'

'Did Betsy say where she was goin'?' Smythe asked anxiously.

Mrs Jeffries shook her head. 'Not really, only that she had a few things she needed to do this morning. She told us to go ahead and have our meeting.'

Smythe started to ask another question, then realized it would be useless. He'd just have to wait till the lass came home to make his peace with her. But cor blimey, he'd not thought it was that big a sin he'd committed. So he'd never told her about all his trips to Australia. He'd told her about one of them. But he knew why she was hurt. She'd told him everything about her own past. A past that had been pretty grim in parts too, and here he was, keeping secrets.

'Can we go ahead and talk, then?' Wiggins wanted to know. 'We learned ever so much.'

'I'll just bet ya did,' Luty muttered. She gave Hatchet a good glare and picked up her teacup.

'Being childish is most unbecoming, madam,' Hatchet chided.

'Being pompous isn't very becomin', either,' Luty shot back.

'Were you able to figure out 'ow to let the inspector know the poor murdered lady's name?' Wiggins asked quickly.

'Luty came up with an excellent idea,' Mrs Jeffries replied. 'We sent him a telegram . . .'

'A telegram?' Hatchet said incredulously.

'From Rollo Puffy,' Luty snickered at the gasp of indignation that escaped her butler. 'You remember him, don't ya?'

Hatchet's eyes narrowed. 'Of course I remember him, madam.'

'Who's Rollo Puffy?' Wiggins asked, 'and why is 'e sendin' the inspector a telegram?'

'He's not,' Mrs Goodge said impatiently. 'We are. We just used his name. Now can we get on with it?'

'That's a good idea,' Mrs Jeffries interjected quickly. It was obvious from the smug expression on Luty's face that she'd deliberately picked this particular name to annoy her butler. Later, perhaps, the women would get the entire story, but for right now, they'd best get a move on. 'Do tell us what you've learned.'

'It were right easy,' Wiggins said. 'We got to South-ampton, lickety-split and then we found a pub where some of the ship's crew 'ung about. The *Island Star* was still there. She's not due to sail for another two days.' He paused and took a quick sip of tea. 'Anyways, at first we didn't have much luck. Mainly we only found workers from below decks. Then Hatchet 'ere,' he nodded toward the butler, ''e cornered a couple of stewards who knew all about Miss Daws. Seems the lady weren't exactly shy. She talked to anyone who'd stand still and listen to 'er.'

'All ya talked to was a couple of stewards?' Luty asked.

'That was quite sufficient, madam,' Hatchet sniffed.

'Not only were they able to tell us quite a bit about the deceased, but they also supplied us with several names of other passengers who'd talked at length with the deceased.'

'What, precisely, did you learn?' Mrs Jeffries asked. Honestly, between Smythe's long-faced silence over Betsy, Luty and Hatchet's sniping at each other, and Wiggins gushing enthusiasm, they weren't getting anywhere.

'For starters,' Smythe said glumly, 'We found out how the victim is connected to Sheridan Square. Mirabelle Daws is the sister to Mrs Eldon Prosper.'

'Very good work, gentleman,' Mrs Jeffries said. Now they were starting to get somewhere. 'At least now we know where to focus our investigation. Odd that she didn't tell the inspector her sister was expected and hadn't arrived.'

'It gets even stranger,' he said. 'Mirabelle Daws told everyone aboard the ship that the family's fortunes had changed and they'd never have to serve anyone again.'

'Serve anyone?' Mrs Goodge said. 'How do you mean?'

'It seems the family was in service,' Hatchet explained. 'Mirabelle Daws ran a boardinghouse out in the outback, and her sister Annabelle was a lady's maid. At least, Annabelle had been one before she'd married Eldon Prosper. Apparently, though, their brother, Andrew Daws, had struck it rich in mining. Mirabelle supposedly wore a rope of opals around her neck that she never took off.'

'How very curious,' Mrs Jeffries murmured. 'There

wasn't any jewelry found on her when she was killed. Perhaps this will turn out to be a simple robbery after all.'

'If it were just a simple robbery,' Mrs Goodge pointed out, 'why go to all the trouble of lockin' the woman in that garden? Like we discussed before, that took some doing.' She shook her head vehemently. 'It weren't no robbery. It were murder and whoever done it couldn't resist pinching the opals. How much would they be worth?'

'A lot,' Smythe said bluntly. 'It weren't just opals on this necklace. There were diamonds, too, and accordin' to what the stewards said, the two center ones were bigger than currants. I'd say Mirabelle Daws was wearing a fortune around her neck and the silly woman let herself be lured out in the middle of the night to meet her killer.'

'Lured?' Mrs Goodge repeated. 'How do you know that? She might have been forced out.'

'I hardly think so ma'am,' Hatchet said. 'From what we learned of Miss Daws, the only way she could have been forced to do anything would have been at gunpoint. She left the vessel of her own free will.'

'What time was this?' Mrs Goodge asked.

'An hour after the vessel docked,' Hatchet replied. 'That would have been around six in the evening the night that she was murdered.'

'So she got from Southampton to Sheridan Square in the space of what, ten hours?' Mrs Jeffries drummed her fingers lightly against the tabletop. 'How? And where is her luggage?'

'We don't know,' Smythe admitted. 'Not yet

82

anyway. And I didn't think to ask that cabbie I talked to if she had any when he picked her up.'

'We'll find out,' Luty said confidently. 'We always do. Now what were those names you fellers got hold of? Come on, give. The rest of us want somethin' to do here.'

Hatchet nodded. 'Miss Daws was supposedly quite friendly with a woman named Judith Brinkman. She lives in a small village named Boreham outside of Chelmsford. She ought to be easy enough to find.'

'The other one she were well acquainted with was a young man named Oscar Denton,' Wiggins offered. 'He'll be easy to find as well; he lives over the family business. An estate agency over on Cormand Lane near Bond Street.'

'Gracious, you have done very well indeed,' Mrs Jeffries said. In truth, she wasn't quite sure what to do next. They'd gone from having no clues to having almost more than they could cope with.

'That's not all,' Smythe said. 'We got the names of a couple of other people who were hangin' about the woman as well. Lady Henrietta Morland and her butler were all over her, accordin' to the stewards. We ought to look them up too.'

'You're back, Inspector.' Mrs Prosper didn't look pleased at the sight of the two policemen sitting in her drawing room.

Witherspoon and Barnes both rose to their feet. Neither man looked forward to what they had to do next. 'Yes, I'm afraid we are. Uh, Mrs Prosper, is your husband at home?'

83

'He's in his study. I've already called him,' she said calmly. 'Was there some reason you needed to speak with him? He wasn't even here the night that poor woman was killed.'

'We know, ma'am,' the inspector replied. He broke off as the door opened and a tall, slender gentleman of late middle age came into the room.

'Good day, sirs, I'm Eldon Prosper.' His face was long and bony, his eyes a pale gray and his hair, what there was left of it, heavily sprinkled with gray.

The inspector introduced himself and his constable. 'We wanted you to be here, sir, because we may have some very unfortunate news for your wife.'

'Unfortunate?' Prosper said. 'I don't understand?'

'Do you have a sister, Mrs Prosper?' Constable Barnes asked. She looked puzzled. 'A sister. Yes, I do, but she lives in Australia.'

'You weren't expecting her for a visit?' Witherspoon prodded. He wanted to make sure he got this part perfectly clear. It could have a great deal of bearing on the case.

'Not in the immediate future,' Mrs Prosper replied. 'Why? What on earth are you getting at?'

'I'm afraid we've reason to believe that the woman . . . uh . . . we think perhaps that the victim found in Sheridan Square might have been Miss Mirabelle Daws.'

Stunned, Annabelle Prosper gaped at them for a few moments. 'That's impossible. My sister is in Australia. What would she be doing in Sheridan Square? I'd have known if she was here.'

'Nevertheless,' the inspector insisted. 'We must ask you to accompany us . . .'

'For God's sake, man,' Eldon Prosper exclaimed. 'Even if that dead woman is Mirabelle, you've no reason to arrest my wife.'

'We're not arresting her, sir, we're asking her to accompany us to the hospital morgue,' Witherspoon explained. 'We do need a positive identification.'

Mrs Prosper had gone completely pale. 'This is absurd. I tell you my sister is in Australia.'

'But we'd best go with them, dearest,' Prosper said gently. He patted his wife's arm. 'We must make sure.'

She looked at the hand on her arm and then slowly raised her eyes to meet her husband's gaze. 'Of course, Eldon,' she murmured. 'I suppose I'd better go with them. But my sister is in Australia. This is all a mistake.'

'If you think it'll be too difficult, ma'am,' Witherspoon said, 'we have contacted the shipping company. They're sending over the ship's purser. He could identify the victim if you think you'll be unable to face it.'

'The ship's purser?' she muttered. 'What ship?'

Witherspoon felt terribly sorry for the poor woman. She looked absolutely dazed. 'From the *Island Star*, ma'am. We think that's the vessel your sister took from Australia to England. Luckily, the ship hasn't sailed yet.'

'I see,' she murmured. She took a long, deep breath and stared off blindly through the front window.

'Shall I call for your maid or Marlena?' Eldon

Prosper asked his wife anxiously. 'Would you like one of them to accompany us?'

She straightened her spine and took another slow, deep breath and then stepped away from him. 'That won't be necessary. I'm quite all right. Wait here and I'll be right back. I'll just get my things.'

As soon as she'd left, Prosper turned and glared at the two policemen. 'This is unspeakably cruel. I'll not have my wife upset.'

'We're not doing it deliberately, sir,' Witherspoon pointed out. 'And we did give your wife an alternative to actually viewing the body. The ship's purser can identify Mirabelle Daws.'

'Even if this woman is Mirabelle Daws,' Prosper shot back. 'It could well be nothing more than a coincidence of names, sir.'

Witherspoon hadn't thought of that. 'Yes, I suppose it could,' he mumbled. 'But two women, both of them from Australia and both of them having the name Daws?'

'Mirabelle is quite an unusual name, though. Isn't it?' Barnes said softly.

Prosper clamped his mouth shut and said nothing else until Mrs Prosper, now wearing a blue hat with a midnight blue veil, gloves and carrying a dark green parasol, returned to the drawing room. 'Shall we go, gentlemen? I'd really like to get this over with.'

'Mrs Prosper did quite a bit better than her husband,' Barnes said as he and Witherspoon came out of the mortuary at St Thomas's hospital. 'For a few minutes there it looked like he might bring up his breakfast.'

'I don't blame the poor fellow,' the inspector said. He stopped and took in several large gulps of air. 'It really was quite awful. I don't see how you and the medical people are able to stand these sort of places.'

'Well, sir, I don't have much of a sense of smell.' Barnes grinned. His inspector really was quite a squeamish sort, not that it kept him from doing his duty, it didn't. That made the constable admire Witherspoon even more. It was hard facing things that literally made you sick to your stomach. But the inspector did it without complaint. 'Makes it easier when you don't smell the place. I think that's how some of the doctors do it, too. Old Doctor Potter once admitted to me he couldn't smell much. Not that he was much of a doctor. I'm glad you had Mrs Prosper come in to identify the body, sir. I'd have felt uneasy relying only upon the purser's identification. Not that I think the fellow is lying, but only to make sure we'd actually got Mrs Prosper's sister and not just someone using her name.'

Witherspoon nodded his agreement. 'Yes, er, quite. Do you think she's telling the truth?'

'About it bein' her sister,' Barnes asked. 'Why, yes, sir, I do. At first I thought she was a real cold woman, but the way she hung back and couldn't hardly make herself set foot in the viewing room got me to thinking that maybe I was wrong. It was hard for the lady, sir.'

'It was hard for the purser, and he wasn't even related to Miss Daws,' Witherspoon pointed out. 'He was quite green about the gills himself.'

They'd seen the purser leaving with a police

constable as they were approaching the mortuary room. After escorting the man to the street and putting him in a hansom, the constable had come back and confirmed the purser's identification of the victim.

Barnes chuckled. 'You'd think a seaman would have a stronger stomach, wouldn't you, sir? But it just goes to show that there's no tellin' how dead bodies are goin' to affect people. By the way, while you were talking to Mrs Prosper, Constable Edmunds slipped back and told me that if we needed the purser to give identification evidence in court, he'd be available. He won't be sailing on the ship. The fellow's retiring to his family home in Chiswick.'

'That's good to know, but I don't think we'll need him. Mrs Prosper's evidence ought to be sufficient.' Witherspoon sighed and stopped in the middle of the busy pavement. 'I do wish I knew what to make of it all. Why on earth would a woman take it into her head to come halfway around the world and not even tell her family she was on her way? It simply doesn't make any sense.'

Betsy dashed into the kitchen. She skidded to a halt when she saw that it was empty. 'Drat,' she mumbled. 'And I've got ever so much to tell.'

'Have ya now?' Smythe stepped out from the front hall and into view. He'd been waiting for her. 'Well, I'm glad you've had such a good day, lass.'

'Where is everybody?' she demanded with a frown.

'Out and about,' he said easily. 'Why don't we sit down? I'd like to 'ave a word with you.'

'Mrs Goodge isn't out and about,' Betsy said. She

moved towards the kitchen table, pulled out a chair and took a seat. She was still a bit miffed at the coachman, but she might as well sit down and rest her feet.

'She's out in the garden shelling peas,' he said, taking the chair across from her. 'She's got one of 'er sources lendin' a 'and.'

'Where's Mrs Jeffries and the others?'

'She's out doin' some snoopin' of her own,' he replied. 'Wiggins is up changin' his shirt and Luty and Hatchet are probably on their way 'ere as we speak. Everyone's meetin' 'ere in a few minutes.'

'Good,' she said flatly. 'I've a lot to report. Maybe I ought to put the kettle on.' She started to get up.

'Give it a minute,' he ordered. 'We need to talk. I've got somethin' important to tell you.'

Staring at him, she sank back into her seat. 'All right. Go ahead.'

Smythe wasn't quite sure how to begin. But he knew he had to tell her the truth. If it changed her feelings for him, well, that was a risk he'd take. He cleared his throat. 'Uh, I know you're a bit annoyed with me . . .'

'More than just a bit,' she shot back. 'Just so you'll know, Smythe, I'm furious. I've told you everything about myself, and you haven't returned the favor. I thought you'd only been to Australia the one time. But you've been a lot more than that.'

'Not that many times,' he said defensively, 'but I'll admit to bein' a bit vague. But I had a reason, Betsy.'

'What reason? It's not that I give a toss how many times you've gone. What hurt me was the fact that you'd not bothered to tell me at all, and I've told you everything.' She broke off and looked away as her throat closed a bit.

Smythe's heart broke as he watched her struggle with her emotions. But he knew her well enough to know that if he reached out a hand to her, she might just tear off his arm. He'd hurt her badly and that was the last thing he'd ever wanted to do. 'Betsy, I'm sorry, lass. You're right, you've trusted me with so much of your own life. I think it's time I trusted you with mine.'

She dragged a deep breath into her lungs and turned to stare at him. 'What do you mean by that?'

He decided to plunge straight in. 'I've been to Australia five times. The first time I went there to make my fortune. The last four times I went was to check on my investments. I've also been to America a time or two for the same reason.'

Betsy didn't say a word. She simply stared at him. Finally, she said, 'Smythe, are you sure you're feeling all right?'

It took a moment before he understood. She didn't believe him. 'Cor blimey, Betsy, of course I'm all right. Do ya think I'm makin' this up?'

'No, no,' she said quickly, 'of course not. But perhaps you're exaggerating just a bit.'

He was dumbfounded. Of all the reactions he'd expected her to have, this one had never occurred to him. 'I'm not ruddy well exaggeratin',' he snapped. 'No one goes on a long, borin' trip all the way to Australia for the bloomin' fun of it.'

'No, but they do go for other reasons.' She reached across the table and patted his arm. 'Exactly when did these trips take place? I've known you for four years, and the longest I've ever seen you gone was a couple of days.'

'I went in the three years before the inspector inherited this house from Euphemia,' he yelled. Euphemia Witherspoon had been the inspector's aunt. She'd also been a special friend of the coachman's. She'd left this house and a fortune to her nephew. She'd also extracted a promise from Smythe.

'That's right.' Betsy nodded. 'You worked for Euphemia Witherspoon, didn't you? You and Wiggins.'

'Originally, yes, I did,' he was almost shouting now. 'But I wasn't workin' for her when she died, and it's all because of a promise I made to her that I'm in this mess now.'

'Promise, what promise?' Wiggins bounced into the kitchen. Fred was right on his heels.

'We'll continue this talk later,' Smythe hissed. 'I'd be obliged if you'd keep what I've told you to yourself.'

'I'll not say a word.' Betsy, who was quite enjoying herself now, giggled.

'Am I interruptin'?' the footman asked innocently. He pulled out a chair and flopped down.

'It's nothing important,' the maid shot the coachman a cheeky grin. 'Smythe was just telling me some interesting tales. Right imaginative ones they were, too.'

CHAPTER FIVE

It was obvious to both the cook and the house-keeper that while Betsy's frame of mind was much improved since the morning, Smythe's had taken a turn for the worse. Mrs Jeffries sighed silently and glanced at Mrs Goodge, who shrugged. She took her place at the head of the table. There was nothing she could do to insure that the course of young love ran smooth. These two would have to work their troubles out for themselves.

'I'm glad we're all here on time,' Mrs Jeffries said briskly. 'I've a feeling we've a lot to tell one another.'

'I had the most interesting chat with a grocer's clerk this morning,' Betsy said enthusiastically, 'and I've found out how the murdered woman is connected with Sheridan Square.'

'I know how the woman was connected,' Mrs Goodge said bluntly.

'So do I,' said Luty.

'Me too, I'm afraid,' Hatchet added.

'All of you know?' Betsy asked in exasperation.

'I'm afraid so, Betsy,' Mrs Jeffries said apologetically. 'Once we had the name . . .'

'Yes, yes, I know.' The maid waved her hand dismissively. 'Once we had the name, finding out the connection was easy. But I bet you didn't know that that Annabelle Daws Prosper used to be a lady's maid.'

Mrs Jeffries winced guiltily.

Betsy gasped. 'How did you find that out?'

'I had rather a long chat with a Miss Varsleigh. She's the housekeeper for Colonel Bartell, one of the other residents of Sheridan Square. I saw her leaving the Bartell residence and followed her. When she went into the Lyons Tea Shop on Oxford Street, it seemed far too good an opportunity to miss. As a matter of fact, Betsy, we ought to bring you up to speed on what Hatchet, Smythe and Wiggins learned in Southampton. You missed this morning's meeting.' Quickly and efficiently she told the maid what they'd learned.

'Oh?' Betsy frowned thoughtfully. 'I see.'

'What else did this Miss Varsleigh tell you?' Hatchet asked the housekeeper.

'Quite a bit, actually,' Mrs Jeffries mused. 'I don't know how much of it is pertinent to our case, but she gave me an enormous earful regarding the Prosper family. But I really think we ought to let Betsy say her piece first, she was out awfully early this morning.'

'Thank you,' Betsy said. 'As I was saying, I found out that Mrs Prosper used to be a lady's maid when she lived in Australia.'

'We know that,' Wiggins said. 'What we don't know is 'ow she end up bein' the mistress of that big 'ouse?'

'If you'll let me finish, you'll find out,' she said tartly. 'Mrs Prosper worked for a family called

93

Moulton before she married Mr Prosper. No one knows how it happened, but Annabelle Daws, as she was then, started corresponding with Eldon Prosper. He'd made a fortune in copper and pipe fittings. He's got a factory up in Lancashire somewhere. But despite all his money and success, he was a lonely sort and wanted to get married . . .'

'Couldn't 'e find someone 'ere to marry 'im?' Wiggins asked.

'Apparently not,' she snapped.

'But if 'e 'ad all this money and all,' the lad protested. 'Why'd 'e 'ave to bring someone all the way from Australia?'

'There could be any of a dozen reasons for his actions,' Mrs Jeffries said firmly. 'Now do let Betsy finish.'

'Thank you.' Betsy nodded at the housekeeper. 'As I was saying, after a year or so of regular correspondence, Eldon Prosper proposed to Annabelle Daws.'

'Did he care that she was a maid?' Luty asked curiously. 'Not that there's anything wrong with bein' a maid,' she said quickly, 'but you English put a lot of store in things like that. I guess I'm wondering why with all his money he wanted a woman that had to work fer her living?'

'That's a good question,' Mrs Jeffries said thoughtfully. She looked at Betsy. 'Do you have an answer?'

'Actually.' She smiled proudly, pleased that she'd had the foresight to find out the right information. 'I do. Prosper wasn't born wealthy, and he's got plenty, but he's not so rich that he looks down his nose at them that's had to work. Besides, he was absolutely captivated by Annabelle's letters. He's supposedly a very sensitive man. He fell in love with her because they both shared a love of poetry and nature. She might have been a maid, but she is educated and can read and write. Apparently the Daws family fortunes tend go up and down, and both the girls managed to get some education when times were good.'

'That's what I heard too,' Mrs Goodge put in. 'From my sources, that is. Prosper was besotted with her from the letters. But even when he proposed, it took a few months before she agreed to leave her family and come here to marry him.'

'Really?' Betsy said. 'I didn't know that part.'

'I only know about it because my sources knew more about the family that Annabelle Daws worked for than they did about her,' the cook replied.

'Would you like to explain that?' Luty demanded.

Mrs Goodge reached for the teapot and poured herself a second cup. 'Like the rest of you have found out, once we had the victim's name, the connection to Sheridan Square was easy. But the only thing my sources knew about Annabelle Prosper was that she'd once worked for Henry and Abigail Moulton. Mrs Moulton was one of Lord Tanner's nieces, you know. Henry and Abigail had gone to Australia to work for his family business, and it hadn't turned out well at all. There was right old scandal at the time, that's how my sources knew the maid's name, ya see.'

'No, I'm afraid I don't,' Mrs Jeffries said quickly. Sometimes the cook had a tendency to assume that all of them were as familiar with the British upper class and their comings and goings as she was.

'Henry Moulton was accused of embezzling money from the business. His family would have hushed it up, of course.' Mrs Goodge was thoroughly enjoying herself. She took a long, slow sip of her tea. 'But the other principals insisted he be prosecuted. Rather than face that, he put a bullet to his head. His wife was forced to close up their house and come back to England. Some say it was that that caused Annabelle Daws to accept Prosper's proposal. With Henry Moulton dead and her mistress coming here, she had lost her position.'

'She got married because she lost her job?' Wiggins sounded absolutely scandalized.

'Not just because of that,' Betsy put in. She was a tad miffed that the cook had stolen her thunder. 'She wasn't all that young, you know. Besides, what else could she do? Her own family didn't have much, and she probably didn't want to be a burden to them.'

'She didn't end up a burden, that's for certain.' Mrs Goodge chuckled. 'Eldon Prosper sent her a ticket for a first-class suite on the *Island Star* and a bundle of cash as well.'

'How come the gossipmongers know so much about the Moultons' lady's maid?' Hatchet asked. 'That's a bit odd, don't you think?'

Mrs Goodge's eyes twinkled. 'It's not in the least odd when you hear what else I found out. It seems that there weren't even enough money for Mrs Moulton to buy herself the cheapest passage back to England. Annabelle bought her a ticket. The two women came back together on the same ship. Only before the vessel even got to England, Abigail Moulton had become so embarrassed at havin' to come home and live as a poor relation with one of her cousins up in Northumberland, she got off the ship when it docked in Cherbourg.'

'What happened to her then?' Wiggins asked.

Mrs Goodge shrugged. 'No one really knows. Though her family did receive a postcard from her a few months after she got off the vessel. It was from Italy and said she'd found work as a governess.'

'I guess she thought that was better than comin' back and bein' a poor relation.' Wiggins sighed deeply. 'Maybe she's found 'appiness in 'er new life. Let's 'ope so.' Stories like this tended to affect Wiggins deeply. He had quite a romantic nature.

'This is interestin' and all,' Luty said, 'but we really need to know more about Mirabelle Daws than we do her sister. Mirabelle's the one who's dead.'

'Yes, you're quite right,' Mrs Jeffries said. 'We have to discover why someone would want Mirabelle Daws dead. More importantly, we need to know why she didn't tell anyone she was coming to England.'

'How do you know she didn't tell anyone?' Mrs Goodge asked.

'Because if she had, her sister would have reported her missing when she didn't arrive at the Prosper house.'

'And she didn't do that, did she?' Smythe said thoughtfully. 'Maybe instead of just talkin' to one or two people that was on the ship with Mirabelle, we ought to talk to more of 'em. Seems to me if she didn't write and tell 'er sister she were comin', she

97

musta 'ad a reason. Maybe she told someone on the ship what that reason might be.'

'But we are goin' to be talkin' to the people who were onboard with 'er,' Wiggins reminded him. 'We just ain't tracked 'em down yet.'

'You don't' understand.' Smythe shook his head. 'I'm thinkin' we ought to round up as many of 'em as possible to talk to. We only got a couple o'names when we was in Southampton. Like Luty said, it's Mirabelle that's dead, not 'er sister. We need to find as many as we can that was on that ship with 'er. Someone's bound to know something, or they might 'ave seen something, when the vessel docked. It's a long voyage and there's something about all that water surroundin' you that draws people together. Makes 'em tell things they'd normally keep to themselves.'

'You'd know all about that, wouldn't you?' Betsy gave him a smile that didn't quite reach her eyes. 'Considering how much you've traveled.'

Smythe opened his mouth to protest, but before he could say anything, Mrs Jeffries intervened. 'I think that's a very good idea, Smythe. The only problem is, how do we go about finding the names of the others that were on board with her?'

'I can take care of that,' Luty volunteered.

Everyone stared at her. Clearly enjoying her moment of glory, she grinned broadly. 'The *Island Star* is owned by the Hamilton-Dyston Steamship Line. Jon Dyston was a close friend of my late husband's. All I got to do is ask, and he'll git me a copy of the passenger manifest.'

'And pray tell, madam,' Hatchet asked archly,

'precisely what will you tell Lord Dyston when he asks you why you want it?'

If possible, her smile widened. 'Don't you worry yerself about that, Hatchet, I'll think of somethin'. As soon as we're finished here, we can drop by Dyston's townhouse on the way home. I'll have that manifest first thing tomorrow morning.'

'That would be very helpful, Luty,' Mrs Jeffries said.

Annoyed that his employer had one-upped him so neatly, Hatchet contented himself with a faint sneer and turned to Mrs Jeffries. 'Does this mean we're not to focus on any of the other residents of the square?' he asked.

'Not at all,' Mrs Jeffries replied. 'Contacting the other passengers is a good idea. But as we've learned in the past, we mustn't investigate with preconceived notions. And we must keep in mind that because the victim was connected with one of the residents of the square, it doesn't mean someone else didn't kill her. For all we know, someone from the ship could well be the murderer.'

'If it was someone she met on the *Island Star*, why kill her at Sheridan Square?' Betsy asked. 'Why not just shove her overboard late at night when there was no one about? Why wait until she got all the way to London?'

Mrs Jeffries shook her head. 'I don't know, Betsy. I'm simply saying that we mustn't ignore any possibilities. There may even be someone from Sheridan Square who had a reason to want her dead.'

'That'd be a bit of a stretch, wouldn't it?' Mrs

Goodge pushed her glasses up her nose. 'Not that I've any objections to keeping my sources on the hunt, so to speak. But I can't see that anyone else on Sheridan Square could possibly have a reason for wanting Mirabelle Daws dead. Take that Mrs Isadora Lucas, the widow lady that lives at number two. Why would she want to kill a foreigner she'd never set eyes on?'

'How do we know she'd never set eyes on her before?' Betsy asked as she tossed a quick glance at Smythe. 'Seems to me that half of London's been to Australia dozens of times.'

'We don't know anything as yet,' Mrs Jeffries soothed. Goodness, were they all deliberately being obtuse. 'And though I tend to agree with Mrs Goodge, we must still keep an open mind.' She looked at the cook and asked. 'What did you find out about this Mrs Lucas?' She knew good and well that name hadn't been dropped into the discussion by accident.

'Isadora Lucas hasn't left her house in over ten years,' she replied. 'One of my sources told me she went in and shut herself up after she was jilted by her fiancé.'

'But you said she was a *Mrs* Lucas,' Wiggins pointed out.

'She's been a Mrs for years. She was widowed young,' Mrs Goodge said.

Mrs Jeffries made a mental note to ask the inspector about this. The only thing he'd said about the Lucas woman was that she hadn't seen or heard anything. 'Well, perhaps things will be a bit clearer the more we investigate. Is there anything else anyone wants to add?' She paused and looked pointedly at the men.

'I'm afraid I didn't have much luck with Miss Brinkman today,' Hatchet explained.

'And that Oscar Denton weren't 'ome either,' Wiggins put in. 'I wasted hours today 'angin' about waitin' fer 'im to come 'ome.'

'In that case,' Mrs Jeffries said, 'let's decide what we're going to do next.'

'I'd like to nip back round to the square and find out what I can about the rest of the 'ousehold,' Wiggins volunteered. 'Then I'll 'ave another go at this Denton feller. But I don't think there's much of a 'urry about it. The estate agency were locked up nice and tight.'

'All right,' the housekeeper agreed. 'Don't give up on Denton, though. He is one of the few clues we have about Mirabelle.'

'Does Mrs Prosper have a maid?' Betsy asked.

'I don't know,' Mrs Jeffries replied. 'Does anyone else?'

None of them did.

'I think I'll try to find out,' the maid continued, 'and if she does, I'll have a go at her. It should be interesting to see how Annabelle treats her own maid, if she has one.'

'I'll have a go at the local pubs,' Smythe rose to his feet. 'There ought to be some infomation I can suss out tonight.'

'I thought you and Hatchet was a'goin' to talk to the people Mirabelle met on the ship?' Luty asked. 'Just because this Brinkman woman wasn't home don't mean you should give up. If you're not wantin' to do it, I'll have a . . .'

'Absolutely not, madam,' Hatchet put in quickly. 'I've already made inquiries concerning Miss Brinkman, and I'll thank you to let me continue at my own pace.'

'Meanin' that she didn't want to talk to you,' Luty said gleefully.

As that was precisely what it meant, Hatchet blustered even more than usual. 'Certainly not, it's simply that it wasn't convenient today . . .'

'Bet she slammed the the door in yer face?' Luty asked. 'Not to worry, she'll not be slammin' the door on a poor old soul like me.'

Since that was just what had happened, Hatchet sighed in exasperation and then gave in gracefully. 'Actually, madam, it might be a good idea for you to have a try. While you're doing that, I'll have some of my sources come up with whatever information is available on Lady Henrietta Morland. I didn't have time to make any inquiries concerning her today.'

Luty nodded. 'Suits me.'

'I think I might keep on investigating the others on the square,' Mrs Jeffries said. 'At least until Luty gets a copy of that passenger manifest.'

Inspector Witherspoon sighed gratefully and sank down onto his seat at the dining table. He oughtn't to be so hungry. Generally viewing a dead body put him off his food for days, but for some odd reason, this evening he was famished.

He picked up his serviette and flicked it onto his lap. 'Are you sure I can't persuade you to join me?' he asked his housekeeper as he sliced off a bite of roast beef and popped it into his mouth.

'No, thank you, sir.' She smiled serenely. 'I ate earlier with the others. We were getting a bit concerned when you were so late this evening.'

'Murder investigations are never simple,' Witherspoon said. 'One never knows what's going to crop up next. Take today, for instance. Once we got that telegram, things began to happen quite quickly. Very quickly, indeed.' He told her about his visit to the Prosper residence and then the trip to the mortuary to identify the body.

'How very dreadful, sir.' She clucked her tongue sympathetically.

'It certainly wasn't very pleasant,' he replied, 'but Mrs Prosper managed it quite well. Mind you, the poor ship's purser turned a bit green about the gills . . .'

'Ship's purser?' she queried. 'You mean the purser from the *Island Star*?'

'Yes, we had a bit of luck there.' The inspector smiled briefly. 'The fellow's retired. This voyage in from Australia was his last. He was most cooperative and didn't mind coming in to have a look at the body. We warned him it wouldn't be very pleasant.'

'But if you had Mrs Prosper to make an identification,' she asked, 'why did you want the purser?'

'Just to double-check.' He nodded vigorously and stuffed a huge bite of roasted potato in his mouth. 'We wanted some verification as to whether or not it was Miss Daws. He confirmed her identity. Poor fellow, even with the warning that it wouldn't be pleasant, it was quite upsetting for him. I was quite glad I'd had the foresight to ask the purser for his help. It was a bit worrying whether or not Mrs Prosper was going to be able to go in.'

'I take it she was squeamish, sir?'

Witherspoon frowned. 'Not at first. She was fine until we got just outside the viewing room. Then all of a sudden, she stopped, began sobbing and threw herself in her husband's arms. She made an awful lot of noise, startled the constable escorting the purser out. But to her credit, she got hold of herself and insisted on going in and having a look. Barnes thinks it was the smell that finally got to her. The air does get rather horrid in those places.'

'I see.' Mrs Jeffries nodded absently. She was racking her brain, trying desperately to think of a way to let the inspector know some of what she and the others had learned today. 'Was Mrs Prosper expecting her sister?'

'No.' The inspector speared another piece of beef. 'She says Mirabelle never said a word about coming for a visit.'

'How sad that she came all this way to end up murdered.' She sighed. 'Was the purser able to supply you with any names of the other passengers? I mean, was he useful at all?'

'Quite.' He smiled. 'Miss Daws wasn't shy. Apparently, she told everyone on board with her that she was coming to England to "talk some sense into her sister and make her come home."'

Mrs Jeffries couldn't believe her ears. Inspector Witherspoon had apparently got the jump on them about this particular bit of information. 'She wanted her sister to come back to Australia?'

'Oh, yes.' He nodded cheerfully. 'It seems their brother, one Mr Andrew Daws, had struck it rich in the outback mining. Now that the family had money, Mirabelle seemed to be of the opinion that she could persuade her sister to leave her spouse and come back to Sydney. Apparently, the Daws family doesn't take the bonds of matrimony very seriously.' He sobered. 'That reminds me, I might have to consult with Inspector Nivens on this case.'

'Inspector Nivens?' Mrs Jeffries exclaimed. 'But why, sir? How on earth could he possibly help you?'

Inspector Nivens was one of the few people that the housekeeper actively disliked and, more importantly, distrusted. He'd tried on several occasions to imply to the powers that be at Scotland Yard that Gerald Witherspoon had help solving the heinous murder cases that were assigned him. The fact that this was perfectly true made no difference to Mrs Jeffries or the rest of the household. They didn't like Inspector Nivens one bit, and they certainly didn't trust him near their dear Inspector Witherspoon.

'I need to ask him to be on the lookout for a necklace of opals and diamonds,' Witherspoon replied. 'Mirabelle Daws was wearing it the night she left the vessel. According to the purser, she wore it all the time. But it wasn't on her body when she was found.'

'You think the killer took it?'

'Yes, I don't think he could resist.'

'Then you're leaning toward the idea that it was robbery after all?' she prodded.

'Oh, no.' He waved his hand. 'Someone lured her to that garden, and that person killed her. I think whoever did it simply couldn't pass up a valuable treasure.'

Mrs Jeffries cocked her head to one side. 'You realize, sir, that the obvious suspect is Annabelle Daws Prosper. Who else could have possibly had a reason for wanting to kill the woman?'

The inspector finished off a last bite of potato before he answered. 'I've thought about that all day,' he finally said. 'And I've come to the conclusion that I simply don't know enough to form any theories whatsoever. Mrs Prosper seemed to be genuinely shocked that the dead woman was her sister. She certainly wasn't expecting her to come to England and had no reason to want to murder the woman even if she had been expecting her. Mrs Prosper allowed me to read some of her correspondence from Mirabelle. It was quite obvious the sisters were very fond of each other.'

'Did Mrs Prosper know that her brother had struck it rich?' she asked.

'Indeed she did.' The inspector pushed his empty plate to one side. 'But it wasn't just her brother who'd struck it rich; it was Mirabelle as well. She owned half the mine. Yet I don't see money as motive for murder in this case. Mrs Prosper simply doesn't need it. Her husband is very, very wealthy. Much wealthier than he lets on. He made it quite clear that his wife wanted for nothing. From the way he behaved today, I rather had the impression he was very devoted to her as well.'

'It's a puzzle, isn't it, sir?' She rather thought that perhaps she wouldn't try so hard to share what they'd learned with him. He seemed to be doing quite well on his own. 'But I'm sure you'll solve it.'

'I certainly hope so, Mrs Jeffries.' He looked around the table. 'Uh, is there dessert this evening?'

'If ya keep on starin' at people like that,' Wiggins said to Smythe, 'we'll not find anyone who wants to talk to us.'

Smythe shot the footman a fast glare, realized the lad was right and tried to force a more amenable expression onto his face. He and Wiggins had come out tonight supposedly to find someone at this ruddy pub that could tell them a bit more about the murder. But the truth was, he didn't much care if they found out anything at all. His mood had darkened as the evening progressed. The more he thought about it, the madder he got. He still couldn't believe it. He'd bared his ruddy soul to the lass, and she'd acted like she thought he was telling tales. He elbowed his way through the crowd to the bar. 'Two bitters,' he told the publican.

'This is right nice,' Wiggins said enthusiastically as he gazed around at the noisy public bar. There were several small, round tables with people crowded round them in front of the open stone fireplace. Long slate benches with chairs facing them lined the other two walls and along the bar, the patrons were two deep. It had only been Smythe's size that had gotten them near the bar.

Wiggins hadn't been to many pubs. Truth was, he'd just about fallen over in shock when Mrs Jeffries had suggested he accompany the coachman.

'Grab us a seat at that bench over there.' Smythe pointed to a spot to the left of the fireplace. Three men were getting up and leaving. Wiggins made a run for it. He slid his bottom on the bench against the wall and slapped his foot on the chair opposite, saving it for Smythe. An elderly man sitting in the spot next to him looked up from his tankard and stared hard at the lad but said nothing.

A moment later, Smythe ambled across and handed Wiggins a glass of beer. He lowered his big frame into the chair the boy had saved him. 'See any likely prospects?' he asked absently.

Wiggins was taken aback. He was also flattered that the coachman would ask his opinion. 'Prospects? You mean people to talk about the murder?'

'That's why we came,' Smythe replied. He wasn't at all in the mood for chasing after clues. He was too busy brooding over Betsy. Just like the lass to take it into her head to be stubborn. He didn't know what was worse, his worrying about how she'd take the truth or her not believing him when he tried to tell her.

'You a copper?' the old man who'd glared at Wiggins asked.

Smythe cringed; he hadn't realized how loud he'd been talking. Blast, if there had been a decent prospect around, his surly expression probably scared them off.

'Course I'm not a peeler,' he sneered. 'We was just curious, that's all. My friend and I.' He jerked his head at Wiggins. 'We got us a bet goin'. I say it's that ripper feller up to 'is old tricks, and 'e says it's someone else what done it.'

'It's not the bleedin' ripper.' The old man drained his beer. 'She weren't sliced up.'

'Maybe the ripper's changed the way he does things,' Smythe pressed. 'Besides, 'ow do you know what the feller did to her?'

The man smiled faintly. 'I know 'cause I was there. I work just across the street, and I saw 'em bring her out.'

'If ya saw 'em bringing 'er out, 'ow do you know she weren't sliced? She'da been covered with a sheet,' Smythe goaded. 'They always cover 'em with somethin'.'

'Everyone knows that,' the fellow sneered. 'But I know what I knows 'cause I went into the garden the next day. Soon as the coppers cleared off, Jon took me in and showed me where she'd been killed.' He lifted his tankard and drank. 'There weren't enough blood on the ground fer it to have been the ripper,' he said, wiping his mouth. 'Siler showed me the spot, and there weren't enough blood.'

'Who's Siler and 'ow does 'e 'ave anything to do with it?' Smythe asked belligerently. He couldn't back off now; otherwise the fellow might dry up completely. He'd learned that some kinds of people told you more if they were just that bit annoyed. He also deliberately played up his accent. A working man like this one was far more likely to trust one of his own rather than someone from a different class. Besides, Smythe was beginning to enjoy himself. Acting the part cheered him up a little. At least it took his mind off a certain fair-haired lovely that could drive a decent man to drink.

'He's the ruddy gardener over on Sheridan Square

and a good mate o' mine,' the man shot back. His thick, calloused hands wrapped around the base of the tankard, and his watery gray eyes looked mournfully into its empty depths. 'He could tell them coppers a few things about what's what, but they never asked him much. Just kept goin' on about how many ruddy keys there was to the garden. As if that made any difference. Jon says people are always slippin' in there at night an' unlockin' the gate.'

Smythe stiffened. He'd struck gold. Pure gold. He hesitated a split second wondering what tactic to use now. He didn't want to risk shuttin' the fellow up by sayin' the wrong thing now.

But it was Wiggins who hit upon just the right note.

'It's shameful the way them coppers won't listen to what a workin' man 'as to say,' Wiggins agreed sympathetically.

'More their 'ard luck.' The fellow shook his head emphatically. 'They're the ones that ain't goin' to solve this 'ere murder. Not with the sort of silly questions that inspector was askin'. Mind you, Jon did say this bloke was polite like, better than most peelers. Treated him with respect.'

'Ooh, I'd love to talk to yer friend. I bet 'e knows what's what,' Wiggins said eagerly.

'Maybe you'll get yer chance,' a quiet voice said from behind the coachman.

Smythe turned and saw a tall, gaunt-faced fellow with dark hair and a ruddy complexion standing staring down at them. He was dressed in a dark coat and heavy, black trousers that were creased and stained. He wore brown, workingman's boots.

'You Mr Siler?' the coachman asked.

'Who wants to know?'

Smythe eased out of the chair and rose to his feet. He extended his hand. 'My name's Smythe. Yer friend there.' He jerked his chin at the man they'd been talking with. 'He's told us all about that awful murder over on Sheridan Square. I'd be pleased to buy ya a drink if you'll let me.'

Siler hesitated a split second and then shook the extended hand. 'I'll not turn down a free drink.'

'It's a cheap enough price to pay fer satisfyin' me curiosity.' Smythe grinned broadly, playing the part of a curiosity seeker as well as he could. 'It's not often ya get to meet someone that's been there and seen where it 'appened.'

Wiggins got up as well. 'I'm Wiggins,' he introduced himself. 'And we've 'eard all about ya.'

'Beer or whiskey?' Smythe asked as he started for the bar.

Siler looked surprised at the offer. Whiskey was ruddy expensive. 'Whiskey,' he called before the fellow changed his mind.

'You can get me one too,' the man next to Wiggins yelled.

''E will,' the footman assured him. 'What's yer name?'

'Bill Trent.' The fellow slid over to make room for Jon Siler.

Smythe came back with the drinks and handed them round. Wiggins looked down at his now-empty glass and said, 'Don't I get another one?'

'Maybe later, lad.' The coachman took his seat.

'We don't want you goin' ome all wobbly kneed, do we? Now, Mr Siler, yer friend 'ere,'

''Is name's Bill Trent,' Wiggins interrupted.

''E says you know a lot more than yer lettin' on to the coppers? That right?'

Siler stared at him suspiciously. 'Why you so interested?'

'Just curious. Like I told ya, it ain't often ya can talk to someone who's been to the scene, so to speak.' Smythe shrugged and tossed back a swig of the whiskey he'd ordered for himself.

'Can't blame a man for bein' interested.' Siler took another sip from his glass and then wiped his hand across his mouth. 'It ain't that I know more than I'm sayin'. It's that the coppers ain't askin' the right questions. They was only interested in who had keys to the ruddy garden.'

'That's kinda important, isn't it?' Wiggins asked.

'Not really,' Siler replied. He grinned broadly. 'That garden was very convenient for a lot of people livin' on that square, if you get my drift.'

'You mean there was them that was usin' the place to 'ave a bit o'privacy?' Smythe guessed.

'More than one was doin' it.' Siler chuckled. 'Well, it stands to reason, don't it? If you're a married feller and you want to have a safe place to meet your sweetie, all ya got to do is wait till old Tavistock walks his dog and then nip out and unlock the gate. Late at night, the wifey's sound asleep, the garden's empty, and you've got the place to yourself.'

'Cor blimey,' Smythe said. 'That's a right good little idea. But if these people was meetin' at night,

112

'ow did you find out? No offense meant, but I thought most gardenin' took place during the day?' He wanted to verify that Siler was telling the truth and not just making up tales. Then he'd try and figure out exactly who the man was talking about.

''Ere, you sayin' he's makin' it up?' Trent asked belligerently.

'Don't get shirty now, Bill,' Siler said easily. 'It's a reasonable question. I know about what was goin' on 'cause I saw it with my own eyes. A time or two they left the front gate unlocked when they was finished. Well, I knew that if Tavistock saw that, it'd be my job. I also noticed it almost always happened on Sunday night. So after I found the gate open for a third time when I come in on Monday morning, I decided to suss out what was goin' on. The following Sunday I waited till after I saw Tavistock take his stupid dog walkies, then I used my key and let myself in. I hid in the bushes behind the bench. Didn't have to wait long, either. About half past one, that Mr Heckston came waltzing in as big as you please. Whistling, he was, like he didn't have a care in the world. He plopped down on the bench, and within ten minutes his ladyfriend had shown up.'

'Who was she?' Wiggins asked.

Siler smiled broadly. 'It was that toffee-nosed cow that lives at number six. Mrs Prosper.'

CHAPTER SIX

'She's a right old tartar, she is,' the girl declared. 'You'd think that havin' been a maid herself she'd be a bit nicer, but no, not her. Acts like the bloomin' Queen of Sheba, she does.' The homely young woman lifted her glass and tossed back the gin in a single gulp. It was her third drink in fifteen minutes. 'Wouldn't even have my day out if it weren't for Mr Prosper,' she declared. 'She tried to make me stay in today, tried to tell me that she needed me because of all that bother with her sister gettin' stabbed. But that was just an excuse to keep me at her beck and call.'

Betsy nodded sympathetically. The pub was noisy and crowded and reeked with the stench of tobacco, gin and unwashed bodies. She resisted the urge to cover her nose. She didn't want to give offense. It'd been hard enough to follow the girl into this dirty place without doing something that might cause her to stop talking altogether. Added to that, Betsy's conscience bothered her. She'd bought Alice Sparkle, Annabelle Prosper's maid, three drinks now and,

114

somehow, that didn't feel right. Betsy had flirted with men before to get them to shed their secrets, but this was the first time she'd followed a pathetic young woman into a horrid, smelly little pub and plied her with alcohol. But she couldn't stop now, not when the woman was finally starting to talk. Betsy hadn't been comfortable going into a pub without an escort. But this place was filled with serious drinkers, and no one had even noticed the two women coming in on their own. God knows she'd done it before coming to live at the inspector's house, but that had been a whole lifetime ago.

She sighed silently, knowing that if she'd not been lucky enough to collapse on the inspector's doorstep, she might be in just the same shape as the girl sitting opposite her.

Alice was able to hide her need now. Her clothes were clean and pressed, and she could talk without slurring her words. But in a few short years, the brown eyes would be bloodshot, and she'd be dropping things because her hands were shaking. She wouldn't be working as a lady's maid either.

Overwhelmed with pity, Betsy smiled at Alice and wished there was something she could do to ease her misery. But there was nothing. Maybe Alice might have had a chance at a better life if she'd not turned to drink.

'Why do you think Mrs Prosper's like that?' Betsy asked. 'I mean, it's horrible that it's her sister that was stabbed, but why is she tryin' to take it out on you?'

'Because she's a cow.' Alice shrugged and pushed a strand of frizzy brown hair off her sunken cheek.

'She's mean and nasty. She's got everyone else fooled, but she can't fool me.' She looked down at her empty glass and made a face.

'Let me buy you another,' Betsy said quickly. She raised her hand, caught the barman's attention and jerked her chin at Alice. He nodded, poured another gin and handed it to the barmaid to bring to their table.

'Ta,' Alice said as the woman set the glass in front of her. 'This is right nice of ya.'

'Oh, it's fine,' Betsy replied. 'I had a good night.' She forced the ugly words out knowing that if Alice thought she was a prostitute, it'd loosen her tongue even more. She wanted to get this over with as quickly as possible. Betsy didn't think she could stomach buying the woman another drink. It was too much like drowning a kitten. So she'd pretend she was something she wasn't. She'd noticed that people tended to speak freely around those at the bottom of the ladder and watch their tongues around those closer to the top. She forced herself to laugh gaily. 'If you know what I mean. Do go on with what you were sayin' '

Alice's brows came together in a frown. 'What was I sayin'?'

'That Mrs Prosper could fool everyone else, but not you,' she reminded her. 'What'd ya mean by that?'

Alice sighed. 'Oh, she's got everyone thinkin' she's heartbroken about her sister. But it's all a ruddy lie.'

'Really?'

'God, yes.' Alice continued eagerly. 'She used to pull faces everytime she got one of her sister's letters.

116

She'd read 'em and then rip 'em in half and toss 'em in the trash. You can't tell me she cared one whit for the woman. Why, she almost had a fit when she got that letter six weeks ago tellin' her that Mirabelle was comin' for a visit.'

'She had a letter?' Betsy prodded. She had to be careful here. It wouldn't do to slip and put the maid on guard that she knew more about this murder than she'd let on.

'Oh, she didn't tell anyone about it.' Alice took a gulp from her glass and wiped her mouth with the back of her hand. 'She didn't want Mr Prosper knowin' that family was comin' to visit. Right ashamed of 'em, she was. I could tell by the look on 'er face when she was readin' the letter. She went all pale and shaky like. Honestly, you'd think she'd been born to the gentry the way she acts. It's not as if Mr Prosper didn't know what kind of a family she'd come from.'

'Did she tell you her family was comin' then?' Betsy asked carefully. 'Is that how you know?'

'She never told me anything.' Alice sneered. 'But I can read, ya know.'

'I didn't mean to say you couldn't,' Betsy apologized. 'I was just wonderin', that's all. To tell the truth, sometimes when one of me customers falls asleep, I have a quick look through the pockets. Surprising what all ya can learn that way. Well, a girl's got to take care of herself in this old world, don't she?'

'That's the God's truth.' Alice grinned. 'I started readin' them letters after I saw Mrs McCabe fishin' them out of the trash and havin' a snoop.'

'Who's that?' Betsy asked innocently. She wasn't

sure she quite understood everything that was going on here, but then again, she wasn't used to questioning people at eleven in the morning in a workingman's pub.

'That's Mr Prosper's sister,' Alice explained. 'She used to keep house for Mr Prosper before he married Mrs Prosper.'

'Is she jealous of Mrs Prosper then?' Betsy guessed. 'For comin' and takin' her place.'

'No, she was happier than a cow in clover,' Alice said. 'She wants to go off and do a bit of travelin' with her friend Miss Beems. She couldn't do that while she was takin' care of Mr Prosper.'

'Why not? You just said she were a widow.'

'She's a widow, but she's a poor one.' Alice laughed. 'And Mr Prosper might be a nice man, but he does keep his mitts on the purse strings. He give Mrs McCabe a generous allowance as long as she stayed and took care of him.'

'But didn't he have servants?'

'That's not the same, is it?' she said. 'He wanted a bit of company, said he couldn't live on his own. Mrs McCabe was delighted that he got married. Took the burden off her some. Mind you, I don't think she likes her sister-in-law all that much. But she sure is glad she's there, or she'd be stuck for the rest of her life with her brother.'

Betsy looked puzzled. 'If she was so glad the woman had married her brother, why was she readin' her mail? I mean, that sounds like she was tryin' to git somethin' on her, doesn't it?'

'More like she was making sure she didn't run off

with someone else.' Alice smiled cynically. 'It's not like Mrs Prosper actually loves her husband, ya know. And I know fer a fact that she's got a lover. If I can figure it out, I expect Mrs McCabe could too.' She snickered. 'She probably is thankin' her lucky stars that someone murdered that Miss Daws. Otherwise, Mrs Prosper probably would have gone back to Australia with her sister.'

'You mean she'd run off and leave her husband?' Betsy's head was beginning to spin. She didn't know if it was because of the cigar smoke or the few sips of gin she'd had.

'At the drop of a hankie.' Alice nodded wisely. 'Mrs McCabe weren't worried while Mrs Prosper was havin' her fun with that Mr Heckston. At least as long as she was playin' about with him, Mrs McCabe knew she wouldn't be leavin'. But they had a blazin' old row a few weeks ago, and she's not gone out to see him since. Then when that letter arrived tellin' Mrs Prosper that her sister was on her way and that the family in Australia had struck it rich,' she laughed, 'that put the fear of God in Mrs McCabe. I overheard her talkin' to her friend not two days before the murder.'

Wide-eyed, Betsy dropped her voice to a whisper. 'And what was she sayin' then?'

'She was tellin' Miss Beems that their plans to go off to Araby might be up in smoke. She said that Mrs Prosper was no better than she ought to be and that now that Mr Heckston had told Mrs Prosper he'd not sneak out and see her anymore, she was scared that Mrs Prosper would go back home with her sister.'

'You mean she'd divorce Mr Prosper?'

'Who knows? I don't think she cares all that much whether she's legally wed or not. She thinks she's above everything and everyone. You know, like she's royalty or something. Like the normal rules don't apply to her. Besides, if the family in Australia has more money than Mr Prosper, she'd be gone like a shot. She'd do anything for money, she would. Anything at all.'

Inspector Nigel Nivens deliberately ignored them. He kept his head lowered and his gaze focused on the paper on the top of his desk. Constable Barnes knew good and well that Nivens knew they were standing right in front of his desk, but the bloomin' sod refused to look up.

After a few moments, Inspector Witherspoon cleared his throat. 'Er, Inspector Nivens, I do so hate to interrupt . . .'

'Then why are you?' Nivens asked rudely. He still didn't look up.

'Probably because he has something rather important to discuss with you.' The voice came from behind them and belonged to Chief Inspector Jonathan Barrows.

Nivens's head jerked up, and he leapt to his feet. He was a man of medium height with dark blond hair that he wore slicked straight back from his face. His nose was prominent, his cheeks ruddy and his eyes pale blue and mean-looking. 'I'm sorry, sir. Witherspoon,' he ignored Barnes in his apology. 'Do forgive me. I didn't mean to be rude. It's just I've been so busy. Most of these cases are so difficult, and there's a lot of pressure on.'

Chief Inspector Barrows nodded curtly. Inspector Nivens was a disgusting toady, but the fellow had some rather powerful political connections. The police were supposed to be above politics and all that, but the chief inspector dealt with the realities of life rather than the ideals one spouted for the press. He'd let Niven's obnoxious behaviour toward a fellow officer pass. This time. 'No more difficult than this murder Witherspoon's got. Which brings us to why he needs your attention. You're to give him any help and cooperation he needs.'

'Certainly, sir,' Nivens agreed eagerly.

'Right, then, I'll leave you to it.' Barrows nodded brusquely and went back to his office.

Nivens turned his attention back to Witherspoon and Barnes. 'What did you want to see me about?' he asked grudgingly.

Barnes glared at the man. There were empty chairs on either side of Nivens's desk, but the constable was sure that now that the chief was back in his office, they'd not be invited to sit down.

The large room was relatively quiet, but a few detectives were working quietly at their desks, and a couple of uniformed lads puttered about.

'We'd like some information about some jewelry,' Witherspoon replied. 'We've just found out that a rather valuable opal necklace might have been stolen during that murder on Sheridan Square.'

'Opals aren't particularly valuable,' Nivens said. 'But I'll have my lads keep their eyes open.'

'It's got diamonds on it,' Barnes added. He smiled maliciously. 'Lots of 'em. We need to know if it turns up in any of the usual places.' The constable didn't have to be specific. Nivens, despite being a rude little sod, was enough of a copper to know that the 'usual places' meant anywhere a fence might try to pass stolen merchandise.

'Diamonds?' Nivens was suddenly interested. 'How many of them?'

'They're only small ones,' Witherspoon said, 'but there are quite a number of them. They lie between the opals.'

'How long is the necklace?'

'The purser said it hung halfway down the victim's chest,' Barnes replied. 'So it's a good long rope of a piece. It's got to be worth a pretty penny.'

'So it would seem,' Nivens agreed. 'All right. We'll do some snooping for you. But I've not heard of anything fitting that description being flogged on the street.'

'We'd appreciate any information you happen to come across,' Witherspoon replied.

'I'll have my sources look into it,' Nivens said importantly. He pulled a watch out of the pocket of his jacket.

Barnes fought to keep a sneer off his face. Nivens's sources were generally petty crooks who sold their own out for pennies.

'Anything else?' Nivens looked pointedly at his watch.

'That's all we need. But, of course, we'd be most obliged if you passed on any information you might hear about the murder. Thank you, Inspector.' Witherspoon nodded politely and turned toward the stairs. Barnes, with one last glare, followed him.

Neither of them spoke until they were out of the building and on the street. 'Where to now, sir?' the constable asked.

'The train station,' Witherspoon said. 'I want to have a word with that woman the purser mentioned. You remember, the one who was so friendly with Miss Daws.'

'Judith Brinkman?' the constable queried.

'That's right.' Witherspoon nodded and stepped off the curb. Raising his hand, he hailed a passing hansom. 'Perhaps she'll be able to tell us a bit more about Miss Daws.'

Mrs Jeffries took a deep breath and slammed the knocker on the front door against the wood. She wasn't sure what she hoped to accomplish. She wasn't certain she could even get Mrs Lucas to talk with her, but she felt she ought to try. People who didn't leave their houses frequently saw more than one would expect. Their windows were quite literally their only connections with the outside world.

The door creaked open, and a gaunt, middle-aged woman wearing a maid's uniform stuck her head out. 'Yes? Can I help you?'

'I'd like to see Mrs Lucas,' Mrs Jeffries said boldly. She gave the maid a confident smile.

'Mrs Lucas doesn't see people.'

'Oh dear, that is too bad.' Mrs Jeffries sighed. 'I've come a great distance, you see. All the way from

Yorkshire.' That wasn't precisely a lie; she had come from Yorkshire. The fact that it had been five years ago, when her dear, late husband had passed away was of no consequence whatsoever.

'Are you sure it's important?' The woman asked uncertainly. 'Madam doesn't like to be disturbed.'

'It's very important.' Mrs Jeffries nodded eagerly. 'I need her help in locating someone.'

The woman's thin lips cracked in a ghost of a smile. 'She couldn't help you there, ma'am. The mistress never leaves the house.'

'Who is it, Mary?' a woman's voice called from the depths of the house.

'It's a lady from Yorkshire,' the maid turned and shouted down the hall. 'She says she wants you to help her find someone.'

'Ask her in,' the voice commanded. 'Bring her into the drawing room.'

'That's a bit of a surprise.' Mary smiled widely, stepped back and held the door open. 'Come in, ma'am.'

Mrs Jeffries stepped inside and followed the maid down the hall and into a large, airy reception room. Sitting on the settee and staring at her curiously was a stout woman with fading blond hair, blue eyes and exceptionally white skin. 'Mrs Lucas, I presume,' she asked by way of introduction.

'Correct. Who might you be?'

'My name is Hepzibah Jeffries,' she replied. 'And I've come to see you about a matter of some importance.'

'A matter of some importance,' Mrs Lucas repeated slowly.

'Shall I bring tea, madam?' the maid asked.

'That would be nice, Mary,' she agreed. 'Oh goodness, where are my manners? Please, do sit down.' She gestured to the chair next to the settee.

Mrs Jeffries quickly took a seat. She'd won half the battle; she was inside the house. 'I do thank you for agreeing to see me. As I said, it's a matter of some urgency.'

Isadora Lucas inclined her head graciously. 'I've no idea why you think I'd be able to help you. As I'm sure my maid told you, I rarely leave my home.'

Mrs Jeffries took another deep breath and decided to trust her instincts. There was something about this woman that convinced her she wouldn't be easily fooled. She decided to toss her well-thought-out plan out the window and simply tell the truth. 'Do hear me out, ma'am. I work for Inspector Gerald Witherspoon.'

'The policeman who is investigating that awful murder we had in the garden?' she asked. 'I liked him. He seems a very gentle sort of man. Not at all like what one thinks a policeman might be.'

'He is a true gentleman,' Mrs Jeffries said firmly. 'What I'd like to know from you is some more information about the inhabitants of the square. Specifically, about anyone who might be connected in any way with the Prosper household.'

Mrs Lucas gaped at her for a moment. 'Do they have women police now?' she asked.

'No, no, I'm not with the police . . .'

'But you said you worked for Inspector Witherspoon,' she protested.

'Yes, I know, I'm his housekeeper,' Mrs Jeffries admitted. 'I know this sounds odd, but you see, myself and the rest of our staff are very devoted to our inspector. We like to help him on his cases. Not that he knows we're helping, mind you. But nevertheless, we've found we can learn things that he can't. People will talk to us, you see.'

'People like me.' Mrs Lucas stared at her for a long moment, and then a slow smile spread across her face. 'Your inspector is very fortunate in his staff. Of course, I am as well. I've got my devoted Mary and her sister Hilda to take care of me.'

'And we takes good care of you, ma'am,' Mary said as she came back into the room pushing a delicate wicker tea trolly. The kettle must have already been on the boil and the tray made up because she'd been gone only a few minutes. She eased the trolly into an impossibly small space between the settee and a red, silk-fringed footrest.

'Indeed you do.' Isadora Lucas smiled gratefully at the maid and reached for the teapot. 'Thank you, Mary. I'll ring if I need anything else.'

As soon as she'd poured their tea, she studied Mrs Jeffries openly. Whatever she saw on the housekeeper's face must have reassured her because finally, she said, 'All right, I'll try and help. But I'm not really certain I understand exactly what it is you need from me. When you say you want to know anything connected to the Prosper house, does that mean you want to know which married man on the square is having an improper relationship with Mrs Prosper? Or does it mean you'd like to know that Mr Prosper is well aware of his wife's behaviour but deliberately shuts his eyes to it?'

Mrs Jeffries stifled a feeling of elation. It would, of course, be wrong to gloat. But her instincts had been right! This woman knew a great deal about what went on in Sheridan Square. 'Actually, I think I'd quite like it if you could tell me everything.'

'Then I hope you've plenty of time.' She laughed in delight. 'Because there's plenty to tell. After dark, our garden has more foot traffic than Oxford Street.'

The inspector decided that Miss Judith Brinkman was a sensible, no-nonsense sort of woman. Much like his housekeeper. Dressed in a serviceable lavender day dress and plain black shoes, she sat ramrod straight in the middle of her drawing room and listened to them without interruption. She asked no questions and made no comments. She merely gazed at them with interest as they explained the circumstances of their visit.

'So you see, Miss Brinkman,' Witherspoon finished, 'we'd be most grateful for any help you could give us.'

'That's quite a tale, Inspector,' she replied. 'But I don't know what I can tell you that you don't already know. From what you've told me, the purser has already given you the details of Miss Daws's voyage. I don't know that I have anything to add to that.'

Witherspoon stifled a sigh and glanced at Constable Barnes. He was desperately hoping that Barnes could think of something to ask that might be useful. Something that would nudge the woman's memory in some sort of fashion. They had learned a lot of information about this case, but so far, he'd not a clue as to who the killer might be.

Barnes gave a barely perceptible nod of his head and said, 'Can you verify that she wore the opal and diamond necklace all the time?'

'Probaby even when she bathed,' she replied bluntly. She smiled slightly, and the inspector knew it was because he was probably blushing. 'Mirabelle wouldn't let the thing out of her sight. She wore it all the time. She was terrified someone might steal it or that she would lose the wretched thing.'

'That's not an unreasonable fear,' Witherspoon said.

'True,' she agreed, 'but if she was that frightened of losing it, she ought to have had it locked in the ship's safe. Most of the women on board brought their jewels with them, but we weren't in the habit of wearing them continuously.' She shook her head. 'Mirabelle Daws was a most unusual woman. On the surface, it would appear she simply didn't care what people thought of her. Yet the fact that she flaunted that necklace constantly rather showed that she did care. That she wanted everyone on board to know she had plenty of money.'

'That probably didn't make her very popular,' Barnes muttered.

Judith nodded in agreement. 'She was quite sad, really. I rather felt sorry for her. I tried to help her socially. But it was impossible, I'm afraid. By the end of the voyage, all the decent people on board had completely cut her.'

'Was it just wearin' the necklace that put people off?' Barnes asked.

'No. Most people were rather amused by that particular foible. It wasn't what she did. It was her manner of speaking.'

Witherspoon was incredulous. He knew the English were a tad snobbish, but that sounded absurd. 'You mean they didn't like her accent?'

'Oh, no, contrary to what everyone believes, we're not so horribly class ridden that most of us would ignore someone because of their speech,' Judith explained. 'People cut her because of what she said. People were dreadfully shocked.'

The inspector and Barnes both leaned forward in their chairs. Rather like two old women getting ready for a particularly good morsel of gossip.

'Oh, dear,' Witherspoon said, 'I do hope it won't upset you to repeat it?'

'Hardly, Inspector.' Her hazel eyes sparkled with amusement. 'I spent many years as a nursing sister. There isn't much that upsets me. And apparently there wasn't much that upset Mirabelle Daws either. She talked constantly, told everyone her business and then dared them to disagree with her.'

'What precisely was her business?' Barnes asked. He sounded just a bit impatient. 'We were under the impression she was just comin' to visit her sister.'

'She was,' Judith replied. 'And she was bound and determined to make her sister come back to Australia with her. The fact that the woman was properly married didn't make any difference to Mirabelle. She told everyone that she wasn't going to rest until Annabelle

129

was onboard a ship and heading home. She used to twirl those opals while she was speaking. It would have been amusing except that she was deadly serious.'

'If she was violently opposed to her sister's marriage,' Witherspoon asked, 'why didn't she object before the fact? Why wait until her sister comes all the way to England and then follow her months later to bring her home? It's most odd, don't you think?'

'Not really,' Judith said, 'not when one understands Mirabelle's reasoning. She wasn't opposed to the marriage when it happened. It was only later, after Annabelle had come to England, that Mirabelle decided there was something odd going on. She implied that Eldon Prosper was keeping his wife a virtual prisoner. When I tried to get her to explain what she meant, all she would say was that she suspected that he was keeping her letters from her sister and not letting Annabelle write home.'

'She hadn't had a letter from her sister since she'd been married?' Barnes surmised.

'That's right.' Judith nodded. 'Mirabelle said she'd only received one letter from Annabelle since she'd come to England and that one had been mailed the day her ship docked in Southampton. She was convinced that Annabelle was in some sort of trouble or stuck with one of those monstrous men for a husband. Mind you, I was quite sympathetic to Mirabelle. I suspect if I were in her situation, I'd have done the same thing. Especially if I'd come into a great deal of money, as the Daws family apparently has. But one thing I wouldn't have done was to tell everyone onboard the ship that a man as rich and influential as Eldon Prosper was some sort of animal and that I was going to get my sister away from him if it was the last thing I did!' She shook her head in disbelief. 'For an intelligent woman, that was quite stupid on Mirabelle's part. You can imagine what most people thought. Mind you, it was mainly the men who didn't want their wives around her. I think a lot of the women felt as I did.'

'Do you think it's possible that her attitude about, er, a marriage and that sort of thing might have offended someone so much that they would want to harm her?' Witherspoon thought it a weak motive for murder, but then again, one never knew.

Judith pursed her lips in thought. 'I don't think so,' she finally said. 'People cut her, but they didn't go out of their way to be cruel. I don't think that there was any one particular man that was overly offended by Mirabelle's attitudes. No, I'd say they just wanted to keep their wives away from her.'

'Did you see Miss Daws leaving the vessel?' Barnes asked.

'As a matter of fact, I did,' Judith said. 'There was a real crush on the quay. Relatives and friends were turning up and meeting people, that sort of thing. But as I was getting into a hansom, I saw Mirabelle talking to a young boy, rather I should say a street arab.'

'Do you know where her luggage was at that point?' Barnes persisted.

'I'm not absolutely certain,' she said hesitantly, 'but I think there was a porter right behind her. He may have been carrying her things. She didn't have much, just a large case and a carpet bag. She'd told us she planned to buy some things in London. She spoke to the boy for a moment; then I saw him give her something. Perhaps it was a letter or a message. A few moments later, I saw her moving through the crowd. That's the last I saw of her.'

Witherspoon nodded gratefully. They'd never found Mirabelle's baggage. The shipping line claimed she took it with her when she left the vessel.

'Is there anything else you can tell us?' Witherspoon asked. 'Anything at all?'

Again, Judith hesitated. 'I don't know if this is helpful, but she did tell me she was going straight up to London. The ship docked quite late in the afternoon. By the time it tied up and we passed through the formalities of disembarkation, it was late. Most of the passengers had made plans to stay over in Southampton and continue on the next day. But not Mirabelle. She said she was going up to London straightaway to have it out with Eldon Prosper.'

'I guess she didn't know that he was out of town,' Barnes mused. 'Too bad. If she'd known that, she'd have stayed in Southampton that night, and she'd still be alive.'

'But Mr Prosper was in London that night,' Judith exclaimed. 'I know because Mirabelle had sent him a telegram when the ship docked in Cherbourg. Right after we docked here, she received a reply from him saying he'd see her that very night.'

Witherspoon looked at the constable. Barnes grimaced. They were thinking the same thing. They hadn't checked Eldon Prosper's alibi as thoroughly as they should. 'Are you sure, ma'am?' the inspector pressed. 'We have it on good authority that Mr Prosper was in Edinburgh that evening.'

She shrugged. 'I didn't actually read the message, but I did see Mirabelle coming out of the purser's office waving the envelope about. She was quite pleased. She told me it was all arranged, that she was going to meet him in London. Then she said, and this is a direct quote, gentlemen, she was going to "have it out once and for all with the old bastard."'

'This was right before the *Island Star* docked?' Witherspoon hadn't any idea why this was important, but in the past he'd learnt it was useful to have a person's 'timeline,' as he called it, absolutely correct.

'No, it was right after the ship docked,' Judith answered. 'Mirabelle and I said our farewells, and she went back to her cabin, presumably to gather her things. The last I saw of her was on the dock an hour or so later. Pity, I rather liked her. She was blunt and rather foolishly honest. But she didn't deserve to die alone and in a strange land.' She stared off at the far wall for a few moments and then gave herself a small shake. Turning to Witherspoon, she said, 'I hope you catch whoever killed her. I hope you catch them, and I hope they hang.'

As soon as the inspector and Barnes had gone, Judith Brinkman walked to a door just a few feet behind the area where she'd been sitting and yanked it open. 'Are you all right?'

'I'm jus' fine,' Luty Belle Crookshank scrambled up off the floor of the small storage closet and wiped the dust off her bright orange skirts. 'Jus' fine. Boy, you gotta powerful lot of information outta that woman. I was listenin' so hard, I was fit to bust. Who'da thought Prosper was in town the night of the murder?'

'Would you care to come out and have cup of tea?' Judith invited. 'I believe you must be rather thirsty. You've been in there a good while.'

Luty hurried out. 'I've spent time in worse places. But I am thirsty. Can I help myself?' she asked as she headed for the tea trolly.

'Of course.' Judith chuckled.

Luty grabbed a clean cup from the second shelf of the trolly, filled it with tea and took a long, soothing sip. Then she flopped down on the settee. 'I was parched. Thanks.'

Judith sat down in the chair the inspector had just vacated and looked at the elderly American with wry amusement. The woman's expensive hat was askew, a long line of white dust had settled on the shoulders of her orange and black striped jacket, and there was a smudge of ink on her nose.

'You might want to freshen up before you leave,' she told Luty. 'I'm sorry you had to go into that closet. I'm sure it wasn't very pleasant. It's quite dusty and closed in, but it's only used for storing a few of my late father's things.'

Luty waved her hand dismissively. She'd actually gotten quite short of breath while she was inside the place. She didn't like enclosed spaces. To be more accurate, she darned well hated them. But she'd been stuck. Just when she and Judith Brinkman were fixin' to have a right good chat, there'd been a knock on the front door, and a second later Inspector Witherspoon and Constable Barnes were stompin' down the hall. Thank goodness they'd made a racket loud enough to waken the dead, otherwise Luty wouldn't have had time to beg Judith Brinkman to keep quiet about her and leap into that darned closet. 'Don't worry about it, I'd rather be sittin' on a closet floor gettin' an earful than standing behind a thick oak door and strainin' to hear what was bein' said. I'm real obliged about you lettin' me do it in the first place. Not everyone would be as understandin' as you.'

'Your story was most unusual,' Judith admitted. 'I've never met anyone who helped the police out with their investigations without the police actually knowing anything about it. Most odd, I'd say. But jolly good fun nonetheless.'

CHAPTER SEVEN

Smythe glanced down the staircase to make sure the coast was clear and then hurried across the landing to Betsy's door. He didn't have much time. In less than fifteen minutes the others would be here for their late afternoon meeting. He wanted to have a word or two with the lass before everything started.

'Betsy,' he whispered, knocking softly. 'Are you in there?'

There was no reply. Blast, he thought, frowning ferociously at the door. He was sure he'd heard her going up the stairs not just two minutes ago. Why wasn't she answering? Surely, her nose wasn't still out of joint over that silly misunderstanding they'd had?

'I know you're in there, Betsy,' he said quietly. 'Look, lass, I'm sorry I didn't tell you about all them trips to Australia. But you've got to admit, when I finally told ya about 'em, you weren't very nice. I didn't take kindly to ya laughing at me. Now, if you'll just open up, we can talk about this like civilized people.'

The door flew open, and Wiggins stuck his head out. 'What trips to Australia?' he asked cheerfully.

'What are you doin' in Betsy's room?' Smythe demanded. 'And where in blazes is she?'

'She's downstairs 'elpin' Mrs Goodge get the tea ready for us. It's almost time for our meetin', ya know,' Wiggins replied. 'I nipped up 'ere to 'ave a go at her window. She said it were stickin' somethin' awful, and with this 'eat, she wanted it fixed so she could 'ave a spot of fresh air at night.'

Smythe was incensed. 'She asked *you* to fix her bloomin' window? Why in thunder didn't she ask me?' But he knew the answer to that. She was still mad as spit at him, that's why. Turning on his heel, he stomped toward the back stairs. 'Just like a woman. No matter what ya do, ya can't please 'em. Try tellin' 'em the truth and they laugh at ya. Try fibbin' a bit to keep the peace, and they act like you've cut 'em to the quick.'

Wiggins, who was right on his heels, asked, 'Are you angry about something, Smythe?'

'No.' He started down the stairs, determined that when he saw Betsy, he blooming well wouldn't do anymore apologizing. 'Come on, let's get to the meetin'. I've got a lot to tell and then I've got plenty of investigatin' to do.'

'Me too,' Wiggins echoed. 'I learned ever so much this morning. Almost as much as we found out last night in the pub.'

The others were sitting around the table when they came into the kitchen. Fred leapt to his feet and darted across the kitchen as soon as he spotted his beloved Wiggins. Smythe gave a general nod to everyone and deliberately avoided looking at Betsy as he took his usual seat at the table.

'Leave off playin' with that silly dog,' Mrs Goodge ordered the footman. 'We've got a lot to do today. My report alone is goin' to take a good while, and I've got some sources droppin' by after supper.'

'It sounds as if we've no time to spare,' Mrs Jeffries said. She paused as Wiggins pulled out his chair and plopped down. 'Perhaps we ought to hurry along with our tea.'

'The tea's already poured.' Mrs Goodge began handing around the steaming cups. 'And if you'll give your plates here, I'll fill 'em up.' She snatched Wiggins's plate and slapped two pieces of buttered brown bread, a scone and a slice of seed cake onto it. Then she shoved it back to him and made a grab for Smythe's plate.

'Ta, Mrs Goodge,' Wiggins said happily.

'Yes, I believe that's quite a good idea,' Mrs Jeffries said. 'Who would like to go first?'

'I think Smythe and I ought to,' Wiggins said from around a mouthful of food. 'We found out ever so much last night.' He swallowed. 'Accordin' to what we 'eard, there wasn't any reason for anyone to be scratchin' their 'eads over them garden keys. Jon Siler, the gardener, claims the place is unlocked 'alf the time as it is.'

Mrs Goodge, who'd just shoved a heaped plate of food under Smythe's nose, nodded vigorously in agreement. 'I found out the same thing. My sources seemed to think that a number of residents on the square used the garden late at night for . . . well, how shall I put it? Assignations of an illicit nature.'

'Humph, that's just a fancy way of sayin' there's

some that was sneakin' around and doin' what they oughtn't to be doin',' Luty concluded. 'Course that's been goin' on since the beginnin' of time, I reckon. Now what I want to know is which one was it?'

It was Smythe who answered. 'We heard it was Mr Heckston. He's been carryin' on with Mrs Prosper. They used to meet in the garden after Mr Tavistock had taken his bulldog for a walk. Seems to me, it was right dangerous. I mean they coulda been caught.'

'They was caught,' Mrs Goodge announced. 'By Mrs Heckston. I got this straight from the butcher's boy whose cousin is sister to Mrs Heckston's tweeny. But how I found out isn't important.'

'What happened?' Luty asked eagerly. 'Did she catch 'em in the act?'

'Madam, please,' Hatchet squawked indignantly. 'There are young people present.' He looked pointedly at Wiggins and Betsy.

'Don't be such an old stick, Hatchet. They know what I'm talkin' about.' She waved him off and turned her attention to the cook. 'Well,' she demanded. 'How did Mrs Heckston catch 'em?'

'Not, as you call it, "in the act".' Behind her spectacles, Mrs Goodge's eyes sparkled with amusement. 'She simply woke up and found him gone. The first time it happened, she accepted his story that he couldn't sleep and had gone for a walk. But when it continued to happen, she got suspicious and followed him. I expect that when she saw Mrs Prosper going into the garden a few moments after her husband, she realized he was lyin' through his teeth about being an insomniac.'

'Cor blimey, that was a stupid lie to tell.' Smythe

shook his head, disgusted that one of his own gender could be so dumb.

'Maybe Mr Heckston thought his wife was stupid enough to believe anything he told her,' Betsy suggested. 'Some men are like that, you know. They think you'll believe any old tale they make up.' She hadn't looked at the coachman when she was speaking, but nonetheless, the barb struck home.

Smythe's eyes narrowed angrily.

Mrs Jeffries realized that once again these two were at odds. She didn't mind their little tiffs when there wasn't a murder to investigate, but this was getting very tiresome. She decided to intervene. 'I do think we ought to be a bit more systematic in our reporting,' she said firmly. 'Doesn't everyone agree? Otherwise we're going to be here all evening.'

'Exactly, Mrs Jeffries,' Hatchet said. 'It does appear that several of us have learned the same information.'

'I 'ate it when that 'appens,' Wiggins complained.

Mrs Jeffries didn't particularly like it either, but there was little anyone could do about it. 'Mrs Goodge, why don't you continue?' she suggested.

'Not much more to tell, really.' The cook shrugged. 'That's about all I've heard so far. Exceptin' that Mrs Prosper playin' about is pretty common knowledge. There's even some gossip that claims that the two of them are still seeing each other. One of the maids thought she heard someone in that vacant house on the square. She was sure it was Mr Heckston and Mrs Prosper.'

'When was this?' Mrs Jeffries asked. 'The morning of the murder?'

'It was before that,' Mrs Goodge replied. 'But it was after Mrs Heckston caught them.'

'How does her husband keep from findin' out?' Luty asked, her expression curious. 'It seems to me that there's always them that likes to run tellin' tales on someone. If everyone knows, how come no one's spilt the beans?'

'Someone 'as,' Wiggins put in. 'Oh, sorry Mrs Jeffries, I know it's not my turn.'

'It's all right,' Mrs Jeffries waved him on.

'Well, accordin' to one of the rumours that I 'eard this mornin', Mr Prosper knows and doesn't care. 'E's that besotted with the woman, 'e is.'

'I can verify that information,' Mrs Jeffries added. She told them about her visit to Isadora Lucas.

'Watches out the window, does she?' Luty asked when Mrs Jeffries had finished her recitation.

'Yes, I think she's a very lonely person, but on the other hand, if it wasn't for people like her, our task would be incredibly difficult.'

'Did you learn anything else that may be of use?' Hatchet asked her. 'It appears as if this Mrs Lucas keeps quite an eye on that square.'

'She does.' Mrs Jeffries cast her mind back, trying to recall everything that had been said. Finally, she shook her head. 'She did confirm what Wiggins and Mrs Goodge have told us about Mr Heckston and Mrs Prosper.'

Smythe leaned forward. 'All right, so we know that the Prosper woman and her neighbor were meetin' secretly in that garden. That still doesn't give any reason why someone would want to kill Mirabelle

Daws. From what's been said, everyone knew about the two of 'em, so Mirabelle findin' out wouldn't matter. And 'ow could she find out? She was killed right after she got 'ere.'

Mrs Jeffries was thinking the same thing. 'I don't know. We'll just have to keep on digging. Who would like to go next? Smythe?'

'Wiggins has already told ya what we learned.' He gave them a few more details about the meeting with Jonathan Siler and Bill Trent. 'And that's about all I found out for now. I didn't have much luck this morning.'

He neglected to mention he'd made one of his dreaded trips to the bank this morning. He'd almost escaped, but then Mr Pike, the bank manager, had popped out from behind a pillar just when Smythe was almost at the door. The bloke had gotten clever. Mr Pike insisted that Smythe make some decisions about his investments. Smythe glanced at Betsy and tried a tiny half-smile. She didn't smile back. Blast, he thought. This ruddy money was becoming a misery. First he'd lived a lie with the others because he was rich as Croesus and couldn't let them know it, and now, it was putting a wedge between him and Betsy.

'Wiggins, do you have anything to add?' Mrs Jeffries asked.

'Nah, just what I've already told ya.'

'I might as well go next,' Betsy said. She told them about her conversation with Alice Sparkle. Of course, she didn't tell them where the conversation had taken place or under what circumstances she'd learned the information. Not only would Smythe have a fit at the thought of her going into a pub, but even Mrs Jeffries, for all her liberal ways, wouldn't take kindly to the idea of Betsy drinking gin at eleven o'clock in the morning.

'So Mrs Prosper did know her sister was coming,' Mrs Jeffries mused.

'And apparently so did everyone else,' Hatchet added.

Betsy nodded in agreement. She ought to be feeling better about having been the one who discovered such an important clue. But it was hard to take pleasure in much of anything when she and Smythe were at odds. Plus her conscience was still smarting over her having bought all that gin for Alice. 'Accordin' to Alice, it wasn't just Mrs Prosper who didn't want her sister to come. It was Mrs McCabe as well.'

'That means both of them had a good reason to murder her,' Luty said.

'So it would appear,' Mrs Jeffries said. 'Anything else?'

'That's it,' Betsy said. She cast a quick glance at Smythe, but he was glaring at the tabletop like he was trying to memorize the grain of the oak.

'If no one objects,' Hatchet said, 'I think I'd like to make my contribution now.' He drew a long envelope out of his coat pocket, opened it and pulled out several sheets of paper. Laying them on the table, he said, 'This is the passenger manifest from the *Island Star*. It came over by messsenger while madam was out this afternoon. I thought perhaps we ought to have a look at it.'

'That ain't necessary,' Luty cut in. 'I already knows

what we needed to know about Mirabelle Daws's trip here from Australia.' She grinned triumphantly at her butler. 'But thanks jus' the same fer bringin' the thing. I'd forgotten I even asked for it.'

'You did a great deal more than simply ask for it,' Hatchet said from between clenched teeth. 'You barged in on Lord Dyston practically in the middle of the night and demanded he get you a copy. The very least you can do is have a look at it.'

'Oh, all right.' Luty snatched up the pages and gave them a cursory inspection. 'There, you satisified? Besides, I already told you I've heard plenty about Mirabelle's trip here. I got it straight from the horse's mouth.'

'You spoke with Miss Brinkman, I presume,' Hatchet asked stiffly. He was most put out that his own investigative efforts had come to naught on this case. Most put out, indeed.

Luty grinned. 'Yup. She likes old ladies. She talked a blue streak while I was there.' She neglected to mention that Miss Brinkman had talked that blue streak to Inspector Witherspoon while Luty sat on the floor of a storage closet. Some things were just too undignified to admit. 'She told me that Mirabelle Daws wore that opal and diamond necklace all the time, had the manners of a field hand and a tongue like a shrew.' She proceeded to give them all the details she'd learned that day.

When she'd finished, Mrs Jeffries shook her head in amazement. 'So Eldon Prosper knew Mirabelle was coming as well.'

'And had sent her a telegram sayin' he'd meet her,'

Luty said eagerly. 'For all we know, that telegram coulda told Mirabelle he'd meet her in the garden. He sure had a reason for not wantin' her to come.'

'Yes, it seems he did.' Mrs Jeffries rubbed her chin. 'This is perhaps the oddest case we've ever encountered.'

'You can say that again,' Mrs Goodge agreed. 'I can't make heads nor tails of anything. First the garden's locked and no one can get in or out without a key, then we find that having a key doesn't matter because the ruddy place is open half the time so people can sneak about late at night. Then we find out that everyone knew the victim was comin', and no one wanted her here. And no one's seen hide nor hair of the poor woman's luggage.' She sighed heavily. 'I do hope you've got your thinking cap ready, Mrs Jeffries. You'll have a hard time figuring this one out.'

Mrs Jeffries was thinking the same thing. In the space of less than twenty-four hours they'd gone from having no suspects to having several. 'I'm sure we'll be quite able to determine who the murderer is,' she replied, refusing to take the sole credit for their crime-solving activities. 'It will all come right in the end. It always does.'

The inspector had debated about leaving his second interview with Eldon Prosper until the following morning, but he'd decided against that course of action. He and Barnes waited in the drawing room while the housekeeper fetched the master.

'Inspector.' Prosper strode into the room, pausing

long enough to draw the double oak doors closed behind him. 'I hadn't expected to see you again so soon. Have you found the murderer yet?'

'No, sir, I'm sorry to say we haven't,' Witherspoon replied.

'Then what are you doing here?' He asked. 'I mean, why have you come back?'

'I'm afraid we've a few more questions to ask you, sir,' the inspector said. 'May we please sit down?'

'Of course. Make yourselves comfortable.' He took the chair opposite the two policemen and crossed his legs. 'I can't see how I can be of any help in this matter. Unfortunately, I didn't even know my sister-in-law.'

'We're aware of that, sir,' Witherspoon said. 'But we still need to ask our questions. Now, sir, can you tell me where you were on the night or should I say the morning of the murder?'

Prosper's mouth gaped open slightly. 'I've already told you that. I was out of town on business. In Edinburgh.'

'We know what you've told us, sir,' Barnes said. 'Are you sure you wouldn't like to amend the statement you gave us? It's not too late to tell the truth. We know that you'd reason to dislike your sister-in-law.'

Eldon's eyes widened. 'I don't know what you're talking about. I tell you, I never met that woman. I didn't even know her.'

'You don't have to know someone to want them dead,' Witherspoon said softly. 'You're lying, Mr Prosper. We've had it on good authority that you were going to be in London that very evening. You had an appointment to meet your sister-in-law. She'd

146

received a telegram from you when the ship docked at Southampton.'

'That's not true,' he cried. He leapt to his feet. 'I'll thank you to leave my house. This isn't a convenient time just now. We've got the funeral to plan, and my wife is most upset.'

'Mr Prosper.' Barnes got to his feet as well. He'd been a street copper for years. He didn't like intimidating people, but he could if he had to. 'We can either finish the questions here, or you can come down to the station and help us with our inquiries there. Which is it going to be?'

'We can get verification from the ship's purser and the telegraph operator that Miss Daws received the telegram,' Witherspoon said gently. 'And we can also find out from your hotel in Edinburgh when you actually left.'

Prosper said nothing for a moment. Then he sighed and sat down. 'Oh what's the use? I should have known you'd find out. I didn't tell you the truth because I was terrified you wouldn't believe me.'

'Tell us now,' the inspector urged. 'Tell us the truth and nothing else and I assure you, sir, if you're innocent of this crime, we'll not lay it on your doorstep simply to have the case closed. Now, why don't you start from the beginning. How did you know your sister-in-law was coming for a visit?'

He closed his eyes briefly. 'I got a telegram from her a few days ago. It came to my office. I was quite surprised, really.'

'What did it say, sir?' Barnes asked.

'It was very strange,' he continued. 'I wasn't quite

147

sure what to make of it. Mirabelle insisted we meet in London on the night her ship came into Southampton. I was due to go to Edinburgh for a business trip, but at the last minute, I decided to change my plans. The telegram disturbed me. There was some sort of implication that I was holding Annabelle prisoner here.'

'So you agreed to meet Mirabelle?' Witherspoon pressed. He wanted to make sure he understood the sequence of events.

'Oh, yes, I sent her a telegram care of the steamship line with instructions that it was to be given to her as soon as the ship docked. We were to meet at the Grand Hotel at nine o'clock that evening. I was there, but Mirabelle never arrived.'

'Did you wait in the lobby, sir?' Barnes asked.

'Yes, several people saw me,' he replied. 'The bellman, the concierge, the night porter. A number of people can verify that I was there.'

Witherspoon nodded. 'What time did you leave?'

Prosper swallowed nervously. 'I'm not sure. But it was very late.'

'Was it past midnight?'

'It could have been.'

'Did anyone see you leave?' Barnes pressed.

'Not that I'm aware of,' Prosper stammered.

'So you can only account for your time up to midnight?' Witherspoon said. He didn't like the sound of that. Didn't like it at all.

'I suppose that's correct.' Prosper said hesitantly.

Barnes leaned forward and looked Prosper directly

in the eyes. 'Where did you go after you left the hotel, sir?'

Prosper said nothing for a moment. 'I went for a walk, Constable. As I've told you, this whole business with getting a telegram from that woman upset me greatly. When she didn't arrive, I decided that perhaps her ship had been late or that she'd missed the train or that something had detained her. I'd no idea she'd come to London and gone to Sheridan Square to get herself murdered.'

Mrs Jeffries was in a quandry. They'd learned an enormous amount of information in a very short time. Now the question was how to communicate what they knew to the inspector.

An even bigger question was whether they ought to tell him anything at all. He seemed to be doing quite nicely on his own. She sighed heavily and stared out the window of the drawing room. No, it wouldn't be right to deliberately keep anything from him. But really, it was quite amazing how very different he was from the shy, rather reticient man she'd come to work for over five years ago. Why, she could remember how she'd had to poke and prod and do all manner of things to get him to stick his nose into those horrible Kensington High Street murders.

He'd only been a clerk in the records room back then. She smiled as she remembered how none of the household had known what she was doing when she'd sent them all out and practically forced them to start asking questions. They hadn't realized what she was up to until Inspector Witherspoon was assigned the Knightsbridge murder of that Dr Slocum. Not that Inspector Witherspoon had been assigned the Kensington killings; he hadn't. Pride welled up from deep inside her, her employer hadn't been assigned that case, but she'd made sure he got the credit for catching the killer. Now it seemed as though he was getting quite good at catching killers on his own.

She sighed again and dropped the edge of the velvet curtain she'd been holding as she stared out onto the empty street. Perhaps it was a good thing he'd become so proficient at solving homicides. Mrs Jeffries was beginning to lose confidence in her own abilities to think the solution through.

She wandered slowly over to the settee and sank down. Leaning back against the cushion, she stared at the far wall as she let her mind deliberately go blank. Sometimes not thinking about the case produced the best results.

The soft ticking of the mantle clock filled the quiet room. Mrs Jeffries tried her best not to think, but it was impossible. She wasn't tired enough to relax properly. Additionally, one part of her was listening for the inspector's footsteps coming up the front steps. Why would someone want Mirabelle Daws dead? There were plenty of motives, she told herself. But were any of them strong enough to kill over? Apparently so.

The sister-in-law might not have wanted Annabelle Daws to go back to Australia, but would she want her freedom badly enough to kill? That was a fairly radical way of obtaining one's freedom. Especially as Marlena McCabe didn't know one way or the other that Annabelle would, in fact, go home with her sister. Furthermore, Mrs Jeffries suspected that given Luty's description of Mirabelle's behaviour on the ship, one could make the argument that the last thing any sane woman would want, would be to go and live with a dominating sister who controlled the purse strings.

And what about Mr Prosper? Would he have been that frightened that his wife would really leave? Even in the rough-and-tumble world of Australia, a woman who'd run off from her husband wasn't treated kindly by society.

Mrs Jeffries cocked her head to one side as she heard the distinctive clippity-clop of a hansom pulling up outside. She got up and hurried to the window. Peeking out, she saw her employer paying off the driver. She started for the front door. She'd see what all he'd come up with today, and then she'd have a jolly good long think in her own rooms.

'It's been the most amazing day.' Witherspoon shoved another mouthful of mashed potato into his mouth.

She smiled, waiting patiently for him to swallow. Really, though, he'd done nothing but pat himself on the back since he'd come home. Then she caught herself and realized she was being most unfair. It wasn't the inspector's fault that his investigation was going along quite well while she couldn't make head nor tails out of theirs.

The inspector neatly sliced off a bit of chop and transferred it to his fork. 'Judith Brinkman was most helpful, most helpful, indeed.'

'Yes, it appears that she knew quite a bit about Miss Daws.' She reached for the glass of sherry she'd poured herelf before sitting down. 'Did she give you any indication that there were other people who might have known the victim as well as she did?'

'There was a Lady Henrietta Morland and her butler who were hanging about a bit.' Witherspoon said, 'but apparently, Miss Daws was quite rude to them. Miss Brinkman says they were barely speaking by the time the ship docked at Cherbourg.'

Drat, thought Mrs Jeffries, that was one of the clues that Hatchet said he was going to pursue. He'd planned on going to the Morland home tomorrow. Now it sounded as if it would be a waste of time.

She was convinced now that the killer wasn't someone from the ship. If someone on board the vessel had wanted Mirabelle dead, it would have been easiest to cosh her over the head and dump her into the ocean in the dark of night. Instead, she'd been murdered in Sheridan Square. No one from the ship had any connections to the square, at least not as far as she or the household had learned.

'And then, of course, imagine my surprise when he jolly well admits to staying in a hotel just around the corner from the Sheridan Square,' Witherspoon continued eagerly.

'What? What did you say?' Mrs Jeffries could have smacked herself for not paying attention. 'I'm sorry, I was thinking about what you mentioned a few moments ago. I'm afraid I didn't catch what you just said. Mr Prosper stayed at a hotel? What hotel?'

Witherspoon smiled kindly at his housekeeper.

'That's quite all right, Mrs Jeffries. Our minds do tend to wander as we age. But as I was saying, Eldon Prosper claims he checked into the Webster Hotel on Armond Road. That's less than half a mile from the square. Well, he couldn't go home, now, could he? Everyone, including his wife, thought he was in Scotland on business.'

Mrs Jeffries kept the benign smile on her face with difficulty. She didn't mind the fact that she was getting older, but she certainly didn't have a 'wandering' mind. 'Are you going to verify his statement?'

'Of course.' He waved his fork for emphasis. 'Mind you, I don't think he realizes how much of a suspect he's become. He did have a strong motive for murdering Miss Daws.'

'But, sir,' she protested, 'from what you've said, he had no reason to think his wife was going to go back to Australia with her sister. All he knew was that he'd received a rather odd telegram from the woman. Why do you think that could possibly mean he had a strong motive for wanting Mirabelle Daws dead?'

She didn't really want the answer to her question. She merely voiced the thought to make him stop and think about the situation for a moment.

'Well, uh.' The inspector frowned. 'I suppose you're right. All we've really got is Judith Brinkman's evidence of what Mirabelle said to her. Drat, I do wish she'd taken a look at the telegram . . .'

The inspector broke off as there was a loud knocking on the front door. 'I wonder who on earth that could be?' Mrs Jeffries jumped to her feet and started for the front door.

'Now, Mrs Jeffries, please wait.' Witherspoon tossed his serviette onto the table and leapt up. 'I don't like you answering the door this time of night.'

'I don't like either of ya answerin' at night,' Smythe called as he shot past the housekeeper. He made it to the door first and pulled it open. 'Cor blimey,' he said in surprise. 'It's that Inspector Nivens.'

By this time, Inspector Witherspoon and Mrs Jeffries were both right behind the coachman.

'You expectin' him, sir?' Smythe asked. Like everyone else in the household, he disliked Nivens.

'Of course he isn't expecting me,' Nivens snapped. 'I don't make it a habit to come calling at half past nine in the evening. Now if you'll get out of my way, I'll state my business and go. I've had a long day and I'm tired.'

'Do come in, Inspector Nivens,' Witherspoon said quickly as they all stepped back far enough to let their visitor pass. 'Would you care for a cup of tea? Or perhaps a sherry?'

'That won't be necessary. Please dispense with the pleasantries, Witherspoon. As I said, I'm tired and in a hurry. Let's go into the drawing room.'

'Yes, that's a jolly good idea.' Whirling on his heel, the inspector took off at a fast trot back the way he'd just come.

Mrs Jeffries and Smythe stared at the two policemen for a moment, and then both of them turned and followed. Luckily the direction of the drawing room was also the same direction as the back stairs. Without so much as a glance into the room, the two of them continued past the open double doors.

Smythe paused at the top of the landing and turned to the housekeeper. He jerked his head toward the drawing room and raised his eyebrows. Understanding his silent question perfectly, she nodded once. He took off immediately, taking care to make a racket as he went so that it sounded as if two people, not just one were going to the kitchen. As soon as the coachman's feet hit the first stair, Mrs Jeffries started tiptoeing back up the hall. By the time Smythe had reached the bottom landing, she was right where she wanted to be, standing to one side of the open door. She angled her head so she could hear every word the two policemen said.

'Chief Inspector Barrows insisted I come around tonight,' she heard Nivens say. 'Though in my opinion, it could easily have waited until tomorrow. I don't have all that much news. But then again, he always seems to think your cases are so ruddy important.'

Mrs Jeffries glared in Nivens's direction. His manners certainly hadn't improved any since the last time she'd seen the fellow. Despite her adherence to certain Christian principles, it was people like Nigel Nivens who made it difficult to love thy neighbor. He was rude, obnoxious and desperately jealous of Inspector Witherspoon. He'd made no secret of the fact that he simply didn't believe their inspector was clever enough to have solved so many murders. Well, she thought, let him think what he likes. He can't prove we've been helping all along. Though she rather suspected he'd tried several times in the past. He'd never succeeded in getting the chief inspector to take his accusations seriously.

'Er, well.' Witherspoon's voice was apologetic. 'I say, I am sorry if coming here has caused you any inconvenience.'

'It's caused me a great deal,' Nivens said nastily, 'but I really had no choice in the matter. You wanted to know if any of my people had heard about that opal and diamond necklace, right?'

'That's correct.'

'You're in luck, then,' Niven's voice stretched, as though he were yawning. 'One of them has. I heard about it right before I left the Yard this evening.'

'Excellent, Inspector Nivens,' Witherspoon enthused. 'I certainly didn't expect such a quick response.'

'Why not?' Nivens demanded. 'Unlike some people on the force, I actually know what I'm doing.'

Mrs Jeffries had to restrain herself from rushing in and giving the odious little toad a good boxing on his ears. The nerve of the fellow, insulting Inspector Witherspoon in his own home. Lucky for Nivens, their inspector was far too much a gentleman to take offense.

'I didn't mean to imply you didn't,' Witherspoon hastily apologized again. 'But I must say, don't you think you're being a bit harsh? I think most of the force does a jolly good job. But on to your information. Do tell me the details, sir. Did your source actually see the necklace?'

There was a long pause. Mrs Jeffries could imagine Nivens's expression. By this time he was no doubt gaping like a goldfish, shocked that his nasty sarcasm went right past Inspector Witherspoon. She stifled a giggle. Served him right, she thought.

'No, he didn't actually see it,' Nivens replied.

Mrs Jeffries was sure his teeth were clenched.

'But he did hear about it,' he continued. 'It seems some woman was going round the less-reputable jewelers and inquiring as to the value of the piece.'

'What woman?' Witherspoon asked. 'Did your source get a name?'

Again there was a rather lengthy pause. Then Nivens said, 'Don't be absurd, Witherspoon. The kind of jewelers I'm talking about don't ask that sort of question. Only an imbecile would give their right name when they were trying to fence a piece of jewelry obtained off a murdered corpse.'

Mrs Jeffries winced. Much as she loathed admitting it, Nivens had a point.

'You're quite correct,' Witherspoon replied. 'I wasn't thinking. Did your source get a description of this woman? I mean we must know some details.'

'All I know is what I've already told you. Some woman has been trying to sell a necklace like the one you described.'

'Oh, dear,' Witherspoon said. 'That's a start I suppose, but it's not quite what we were hoping for.'

'I wasn't finished,' Nivens said irritably. 'My source told me that the jeweler in question directed the woman to someone else. A fence named Jon McGee. McGee operates out of a pub off the Commercial Docks. He's usually there most evenings.'

'Gracious,' Witherspoon yelped. 'I'd best get cracking then. It's getting quite late.'

'Calm down,' Nivens ordered. 'McGee won't be there tonight. He's in Birmingham and not due back until tomorrow. So even if your lady goes there this evening, she'll not find him.'

'What's the name of the pub?'

'The Sailor's Whistle,' Nivens said. 'That's all I know. It's up to you to put a watch on the place and nab the woman. You'll have your killer then.'

'I'm not sure I would go quite that far,' Witherspoon demurred. 'We may have someone who has a necklace to sell. We don't know that it's the right necklace, and even if it is, we don't know that the person trying to sell it is the killer.'

Bravo, Inspector, Mrs Jeffries thought. You tell him how a real homicide policeman thinks. He never makes assumptions without thoroughly looking at the evidence.

Nivens snorted loudly. 'Whatever you say, Witherspoon,' his voice dripping with sarcasm. 'After all, you're the great homicide detective.'

CHAPTER EIGHT

Despite Mrs Jeffries's doubts as to the veracity of Inspector Niven's statements, Witherspoon was utterly deaf to her hints that he ought to send a lad down to watch the pub just in case someone trying to fence an opal and diamond necklace happened to show up. As she wasn't supposed to have even heard that conversation, she had to be very careful about how hard she pressed the matter. But it was no good at all. The inspector was such an innocent. He took Nivens completely at his word.

'I'm sure Inspector Nivens doesn't mean to be so grumpy,' he explained as he reached for his coat and hat. 'He's just had a very long day.'

'But don't you think, perhaps, you ought to, well, verify whatever it was he told you,' she'd suggested.

'That's not necessary,' Witherspoon whistled for Fred, who came bounding down the stairs with his tongue hanging out and his tail wagging furiously. 'I'm sure Nivens's information is absolutely on the mark. He isn't the most pleasant of fellows, but I've never know him to deliberately lie. Come along, boy.' He started for the back door. 'Let's go walkies.'

'We'd better make this quick,' Smythe muttered as they heard the back door close behind the inspector. He'd had the others at the ready since Nivens had shown up. It was late and they were all tired, but none of them were willing to wait until tomorrow to find out what had gone on.

'Why?' Mrs Goodge asked. She set a jug of lemonade out on the table and motioned for Betsy to put the tray of glasses down next to it. 'He'll be gone a good forty-five minutes. All he does is stroll across the garden to Lady Cannonberry's. Fred'll get a nice tidbit from the kitchen and our inspector'll drink a couple of glasses of Harvey's. He's certainly taking his own sweet time with that courtship. How long's it been now? Four, five years?'

The entire household had given up trying to rush that relationship. Even though the two involved were very much enamored of one another, neither seemed in any hurry to change the present situation. As far as Mrs Jeffries was concerned, that was just fine. The inspector had a right to make his own choices in his private life. Though she did feel a tad guilty because they'd not included Ruth in this investigation. Their neighbor, despite her aristocratic title, was the daughter of a simple vicar. She'd married well and now that she was widowed and in control of her money and her household, was quite a political radical. But that didn't stop her from being a wonderful neighbor and a good friend to the entire household. She was a fairly good snoop as well, Mrs Jeffries thought. Too bad they'd been so rushed on this case. But that was the way things had worked out.

'Are we ready, then?' Wiggins asked as he flopped down in the chair next to Betsy. He reached for his glass, took a sip of lemonade and then yawned.

'This'll not take long,' the housekeeper assured him. She noticed that Mrs Goodge had dark circles under her eyes as well. The cook needed her rest. Getting up at the crack of dawn to bake and cook so she'd have food to 'feed her sources' was getting harder on the elderly woman than Mrs Jeffries had realized. 'As I'm sure Smythe told you, I eavesdropped on the inspector and Nigel Nivens. But before I tell you about that, I'll tell you the other things I learned during dinner.'

Taking care not to leave out even the smallest of details, she told them everything she and the inspector had discussd while he was eating his meal. Then she told them what she'd overheard from Nivens.

When she finished, Smythe started to get up, but she waved him back to his seat. 'I know what you want to do,' she said, 'but I don't think it's necessary.'

'Nivens hates our inspector,' Smythe argued. 'I wouldn't put it past him to do a bit o' sabotagin'. That necklace might be bein' fenced tonight. Someone ought to get over there . . .'

'I was worried about the same thing,' she interrupted, 'but upon reflection, I don't think Nivens is stupid enough to do something that obvious. He knows the chief inspector doesn't like or trust him, and if it came down to it, Chief Inspector Barrows would take our inspector's word over Nivens's. I think we can safely assume that he was telling the truth tonight. Besides, if he'd been lying and deliberately giving our inspector false information, he'd have been far more pleasant about the whole thing.'

Smythe thought about it for a moment and then sank back down to his chair. 'That's true.' He chuckled. 'Cor blimey, he was in a sorry old state. He were so niggled at having to come round, you could practically seem the steam pourin' out of 'is ears.'

'So what do we do now?' Betsy asked. 'Seems like the inspector's learning as much as we are and doin' it quickly as well. From what he said, there's no point in our trying to hunt down anyone else that was on the ship with Mirabelle Daws, not if no one was even talking to her.'

'Sometimes things aren't always what they seem,' Mrs Jeffries replied. 'As you all well know, we really can't take anything for granted. No one may have been speaking to Miss Daws by the time she left the ship, but that doesn't mean the people on board didn't see something that could turn out to be important.' She'd learned the hard way not to leave any stone unturned. 'I know that Hatchet was going to try and contact Lady Henrietta Morland tomorrow . . .'

''E's goin' on the train,' Wiggins put in, 'and it's a long ways.'

'Colchester isn't that far,' Mrs Goodge said.

'But if it's goin' to be a waste of time, maybe I ought to nip over there tonight and tell 'im not to bother.'

Mrs Jeffries hesitated and then shook her head firmly. 'No. Let him go. He might learn something important. From what we know of the victim, she didn't hide her light under a bushel. She may have given Lady Henrietta Morland an interesting earful before she offended her.'

'But would it have anything to do with her murder?' Mrs Goodge asked softly.

'We won't know unless we ask,' Mrs Jeffries said firmly. They talked about the case for another ten minutes, but it was soon apparent that none of them had anything new to add to the matter.

Mrs Goodge broke rank first. Yawning, she got up and stretched. 'I think I'll turn in. It's gettin' late and I've got to be up early to bake another seed cake. Betsy, could you do us a favor, dear, and tidy up?'

'Of course, Mrs Goodge.' The maid smiled. 'You go get some rest now. You've been on your feet for hours.'

'I can help you,' Mrs Jeffries told Betsy.

But the maid would have none of it. 'You've been on your feet all day too. I can handle this on my own. There isn't much to do. Just a few glasses and a jug to wash and put away.'

As the housekeeper wasn't so much tired as desperate to get to the quiet of her room so that she could have a good long think, she smiled gratefully. 'Thank you, dear. Smythe, will you lock up?'

'Sure, but I'll wait till the inspector's home. I'm not sure 'e took the back door key with 'im.'

'That'll be fine.' She got up and went towards the back stairs.

'Wait fer me.' Wiggins leapt up too. 'I'm knackered. Night, everyone,' he called as he followed the housekeeper.

Betsy picked up a tray from the sideboard and began loading the empty glasses on it. She lifted the jug and peered inside. 'Do you want the rest of this?' she asked Smythe.

'No, thanks, I'm not all that thirsty,' he said softly.

'All right.' She put the jug on the tray and went to the sink. Mrs Goodge had left a sinkful of soapy water ready for her. Betsy carefully popped everything in the steamy liquid. She pretended not to notice when she heard the faint scrape of a chair and a moment later, Smythe standing close behind her.

'I'd like to talk to ya,' he said softly.

'I'm not going anywhere until these things are washed and dried,' she replied.

He cleared his throat. 'There's something I've got to tell ya.'

'Like I said, I'm not going anywhere at the moment.'

'There's nothin' wrong with me hearin',' he said irritably. 'I know what you've said. It's just that I don't want to be interrupted by the inspector.' He reached to one side and whipped a clean tea towel off the rack. Then he picked up one of the glasses Betsy had just washed and put on the wooden draining board and began to dry it.

'What are you doing?' she asked.

'I'm 'elpin' with the cleanup so you and I can go somewhere private-like and talk.'

'And just where would that be?' She plopped two more glasses on the board. 'I'm not goin' to your room.'

'I'd not ask ya to,' he snapped, incensed that she would even think such a thing. 'But there's a whole bloomin' garden outside, and it's a nice warm evening.'

She rinsed off the jug and placed it next to the glasses. 'The inspector'll be home soon.'

'So what?' he said. 'I've got the back door key. He'll come inside and go straight up to bed. He always leaves it fer me to lock up. Now, are you willin' to come out and talk?'

She thought about if for all of two seconds, and then she nodded. 'All right, but not for too long. I'm tired.'

Just at that moment, they heard the back door open. Fred came flying into the room first. He ran over to Betsy and Smythe to get petted. The inspector came in a few seconds later.

'Gracious, are you two still up?'

'We're just finishin', ' Smythe said.

'Don't be too late,' Witherspoon said as he headed towards the stairs. 'I'm sure you're as tired as I am. Good night, sleep well. Come on, Fred, let's go upstairs. We all need our sleep.'

Fred, who was enjoying Betsy's petting, reluctantly followed his master out of the kitchen.

Smythe waited till he heard the inspector's foot-steps fade away. 'Come on, then, let's go.' He held out his hand.

Betsy took off her apron, tossed it onto the table and joined her hand with his. 'All right, I'm ready.'

Mrs Jeffries sighed gratefully as she sank into her favorite chair. She hadn't lighted the lamps, but she'd kept the curtains open. The faint, pale glow of the gas lamps on the street below cast enough light into the room to keep it from being pitch black. She liked the quiet and the dark. It helped her think.

She leaned her head back and began to mentally go over each and every fact they knew about this case. Just the facts, she told herself firmly. She'd pick the other bits apart later. Right now she simply wanted it clear in her own mind what was indisputable. She cringed slightly, aware that she was forcing herself through this exercise because she was concerned that perhaps she wasn't quite as confident in herself as she used to be. Perhaps that was a product of getting older, or perhaps it was simply that this case was so terribly baffling.

She shook herself, determined not to give in to these ridiculous notions . . . she'd go over the facts and then she'd examine the other information they'd gathered, the gossip, the implications, everything. She'd pick it apart piece by piece, and then she'd put all the pieces back together and somehow, someway, some kind of a pattern would emerge.

It always had before.

But first, the facts. She straightened her spine and took a deep breath. Fact, two nights ago an Australian woman who'd never been to England before in her life got murdered in a locked garden. Fact, it happened between four and six in the morning. Fact, the victim was stabbed. Fact, there were no identifying papers on the woman's body. Fact, the woman had just come here from a ship. Fact, an opal and diamond necklace had been taken off her body.

Fact, fact, fact. Mrs Jeffries snorted in disgust.

This was getting her nowhere. She could sit here all night and list facts until the cows came home, but it wouldn't bring her a step closer to finding the killer. Absurd, really. What was she thinking? There was nothing wrong with her mind, and there was nothing wrong with this investigation. They simply hadn't found the key yet. But she would, oh yes, she promised herself, she would.

She relaxed back in her chair and instead of keeping her attention focused on the facts of the case, she let her mind drift where it would. Bits and pieces swam in and out of her consciousness, and she didn't try to put them in any proper order; she simply let them come as they would.

Eldon Prosper hadn't been in Edinburgh on the night of the murder. He had a reason to want Mirabelle dead, too. He was scared that with her newfound wealth she'd convince Annabelle to go back to Australia. But was he really that frightened of such a thing? Frightened enough to kill? And why was Mirabelle so set on coming to 'rescue' her sister in the first place? She had no real evidence that Annabelle was being treated cruelly. Had she? And what about Annabelle Prosper's affair with her neighbor, Heckston? Why hadn't Prosper put a stop to that if he was so frightened of losing his wife? Apparently it was finally Mrs Heckston who'd put a stop to it.

Mrs Jeffries sat straight up in her chair. Good gracious, why hadn't she thought of it before? It was as plain as the nose on your face. Without thinking – for if she thought about it, she might not do it – she got up from her chair and dashed out of the room.

Hurrying down a short flight of stairs, she came to a halt outside Inspector Witherspoon's door. She knocked. 'Inspector, I'd like to have a quick word with you.'

The door opened a crack and Witherspoon, minus his spectacles and with a nightcap on, stuck his head out. 'Is something wrong, Mrs Jeffries?'

'No, sir,' she smiled reassuringly. 'It was just something you said, sir. Goodness, you are a sly one, sir. I mean I'd no idea you were going to send the investigation in that direction. Well done, sir. Well done, indeed. I'd have never thought of doing something that clever.'

'Er, uh, thank you, Mrs Jeffries.' He gave her a thin, worried smile. 'But I'm not sure I know exactly what you're referring to. I can't think of anything I said tonight. . . .'

'It was what you didn't say, sir,' she said, beaming proudly at him. 'Come now, sir. Do confess, or I shall never get any sleep.'

'Er, I'm still rather unsure of what you could possibly mean . . .'

'Now, now, sir. Don't be coy with me.' She chuckled indulgently. 'Surely you're thinking what I'm thinking. Annabelle Prosper and Mirabelle Daws were sisters. Like most sisters, I suspect they resembled each other somewhat.'

Witherspoon thought for a moment. Except for the fact that Mirabelle had been a distinctly chalky-white color when he'd seen her, there was a resemblance between the two women. 'Yes, they were the same height and build,' he said. His mind was trying to catch on to what Mrs Jeffries was saying. Drat, he hated it when he'd been brilliant and then forgotten about it.

'Then of course, sir, you're going to do the obvious, aren't you? You're going to find out if Mirabelle Daws was the real victim.'

'The real victim?' he repeated.

She clasped her hands together excitedly. 'I knew it. I knew I was right and that I'd guessed what you're going to do next. You're going to ask about and find out if anyone had a reason to want Annabelle Daws Prosper dead.'

The inspector's jaw dropped, and then he quickly clamped his mouth shut. 'Well, yes, you're right, Mrs Jeffries. That's precisely what I'm going to do. I ought to have known you'd be onto my tricks.'

'Excellent, sir.' She smiled broadly. 'Thank you so much for telling me. Now I can sleep well tonight,' she waved good night and hurried back to her rooms.

At least now she'd have him asking the right questions of the servants and the local residents, she thought as she quietly opened her door and stepped inside. It shouldn't be too long before the inspector discovered, as they had, that Annabelle Daws Prosper used the garden quite frequently to meet her lover. She shook her head in disgust as she sank down in her chair again. She'd been so blind when the real answer might be right under her nose. Mirabelle Daws, despite the unusual circumstances that brought her to Sheridan Square at that time of night, might not have been the real victim.

No one had a motive to murder her. Yet a good

number of people might have wanted Annabelle dead; Mrs Heckston, Mr Heckston, or even the woman's own husband. Perhaps he was tired of being cuckolded. Killing the wrong woman would be an easy mistake to make. Mrs Jeffries knew that for a fact. It had happened at least twice just on the cases they'd investigated.

Smythe and Betsy sat at the wooden bench under the oak tree in the middle of the garden. It was a quiet, secluded place, perfect for sweethearts. A luminous moon peeked out from behind the branches of the tree, the scent of lavender and summer roses filled the air and in the distance, a night bird sang. But neither Betsy nor Smythe noticed the beauty of the summer night.

They were both too scared.

She was afraid Smythe was going to tell her he wasn't sweet on her anymore, and Smythe was terrified that once she knew the truth about his past, she'd feel differently about him.

'Go on, then,' she said. She smoothed her skirt over her lap and then twined her hands together to keep them from shaking. 'You said you wanted to talk.'

'I'm not sure where to begin,' he said softly.

'Start at the beginnin',' she advised. 'That's what Mrs Jeffries always tells us.'

'Yeah, I reckon that's as good a place as any.' He cleared his throat. 'All right, then. Do you remember when you first came to the inspector's house?'

'I didn't exactly come there,' she reminded him. 'It was more like I collapsed on his doorstep.' The memory was a hard and painful one, but she didn't shrink from it. Her sense of self, of pride, had grown greatly in the past few years. Perhaps it was because for the first time in her life, people she admired seemed to think she was worth something. She'd finally decided that having been born and raised in the poorest part of London wasn't anything to be ashamed of. She hadn't asked to go hungry or watch her younger sister die from starvation. That's what people didn't understand about being poor. It's not a condition that you decide upon. It's something that's thrust upon you, like the color of your hair or eyes. Her people had been decent and hardworking. Both her parents had labored long and hard to take care of their family. But they'd died, and she'd been faced with some ugly choices. Just when life had seemed the worst for her, just when it seemed there was no hope or mercy or compassion for people like her, she'd stumbled onto Inspector Witherspoon's door stoop.

'Sometimes I wonder how my life would have turned out if I'd sat down on Mrs Collier's doorstep,' Betsy mused. She was referring to one of the inspector's neighbors. 'She's not a bad woman, but she'd have shooed me away, not taken me in like Inspector Witherspoon did. I was lucky.'

'We were lucky, Betsy,' he told her softly. 'You were sick and half starved, but so stubborn about earnin' your keep that you tried to get up off your sickbed and help Mrs Jeffries scrub floors. I remember how she had to give ya a right good tongue-lashin' to get ya back to bed.'

'She was wonderful to me,' Betsy said. 'She talked

the inspector into giving me a position, helped me learn how to speak properly and most importantly made me think I was worth something.' She stopped and gave herself a small shake. This wasn't about her. 'Of course I remember coming here. What of it?'

'Mrs Jeffries hadn't been here long, as the inspector 'ad inherited the place from his Auntie Euphemia.' Smythe said.

'I know that,' she said. 'You and Wiggins both worked for her, didn't you? Come on now, Smythe, what's this all about? Are you still annoyed with me because I didn't believe that silly story you was tryin' to tell me the other day?'

'It weren't a silly story, lass,' he said calmly. 'It were the truth. I wished you'da listened then. If you 'ad, this wouldn't be so hard.'

Betsy said nothing. She simply stared out into the the night. In her heart of hearts she'd known he was telling the truth. He wasn't a liar. And in one part of her mind, she'd suspected there was more to him than he'd let on. To begin with, there were all those gifts everyone in the household received. Like when she lost her best pair of gloves this winter and then she'd found an even better pair lying out on her bed. And Mrs Goodge's expensive medicine for her rheumatism. New bottles were always popping up in her room. No matter how many silly poems he wrote, Wiggins always had a fresh supply of nice notepaper. Even Mrs Jeffries wasn't left out. The gift giver always made sure that she had the latest volume of Mr Walt Whitman's poems.

She bit her lip. The clues had been right under

172

her nose. She just hadn't wanted to see them. Everyone in the household received these gifts, except Smythe. And there were other things as well, like the times she'd seen him going through the post when he thought no one was looking. There'd always be a big white envelope for him. An envelope he'd hide in his pocket when he heard her coming. There had been so many things she could have asked him about. So many times when she could have confronted him about all the little mysteries surrounding him, but she hadn't. She hadn't wanted to admit it because admitting it would change things. She didn't want things to change.

'I've got lots of money, Betsy,' he continued, when she didn't speak. 'More than enough to take care of both of us for the rest of our lives.'

'Are you rich?' she asked.

'Yeah.' He licked his suddenly dry lips. She didn't look pleased. 'I can give you anything you want, buy you a big house, we can travel, we can do whatever we want.'

'I see.' She knew that she ought to be happy. The man she cared about was telling her she'd never have to worry about being poor again. But somehow, all she felt was a sharp, searing pain in her heart. She swallowed the sudden lump in her throat. 'I want things to be the way they were. You've lied to me all these years. You've lied to all of us. Why? Was it to make us look like fools?'

His heart broke as he heard the ragged misery in her voice. 'Never, lass. It was never that. I never meant fer it to 'appen this way. You've got to believe me.'

'How can I believe someone who's just admitted he's lied to me since the day we met?'

'I never meant fer it to happen,' he continued doggedly. 'I wasn't goin' to stay. I only stayed because I promised Euphemia I'd hang about a bit and make sure the inspector got settled in all right. He'd never had a big house or any money. So I stayed until after Mrs Jeffries come and then you came and then before I knew it, we was out investigatin' murders and actin' like a family.'

'But you still could have told us,' Betsy insisted doggedly.

'You'd have treated me differently if I'd said anything,' he insisted.

'We wouldn't. Luty Belle's got money, and we don't treat her any differently.'

'Only because you've always known she had money,' he argued. 'If I'd come out and told everyone, you'd 'ave all acted like I didn't have a right to be here. Like I was takin' a good job away from some poor bloke that really needed it. I've 'eard the way you and Wiggins go on about that sort of thing, about people takin' jobs when they don't have to have one. I didn't want you turnin' on me. Not after I'd come to care for ya.'

She said nothing. In the pale light, Smythe could see her expression. Her face seemed carved of stone. He wished she'd scream or cry or call him names. Temper or tears, he could handle that. Anything but this awful silence. 'Say something,' he begged.

With a barely perceptible nod, she shook her head as though she were shaking herself out of a dream.

'What is there to say? You're rich. I'm poor. You've stayed on at the house because it was comfortable for you, I suppose. I don't know. I don't think I know anything anymore.'

It was the God's truth. Betsy's world had suddenly started to collapse upon her. 'If I can't trust you,' she mused, 'who on earth can I trust?' There was one part of her that wondered if he'd not told her the truth as a kind of test. To make sure she really cared about him and not his money. Maybe when she could feel something again, she'd get angry over that. She'd not made him jump through any hoops to win her affections. She couldn't understand why she was so hurt. Most women would be dancing for joy to find out that a man who was sweet on them was rich as sin, but she wasn't. Perhaps it was because in a life of hard times, she'd learned to hold herself back, to keep her feelings to herself. That was how she'd survived the awful streets of the East End.

But she'd opened herself to Smythe, shared things with him she'd never told another living soul, and now he was telling her he'd been lying to her for almost five years. It hurt. It hurt so much that it was almost hard to breathe. 'I've got to go in now.' She started to get up, but he placed his big hand on her arm and pulled her back down beside him.

'Don't hate me, lass,' he whispered. 'For all my money, it'd be worth nothin' if I lost you.'

She looked down at his hand. 'I don't think I hate you,' she mumbled.

'But what I've told ya has changed yer feelings for me, hasn't it?' he asked. He prayed it wasn't true. But he was enough of a realist to know that this particular prayer didn't have a hope in Hades of being answered.

'I don't know how I feel,' she admitted truthfully. She pulled away from him and stood up. She wasn't a fool, and she wasn't stupid enough to let hurt feelings and injured pride stand between her and a man she'd come to care deeply about. 'I just don't know.'

He threw caution to the winds. He loved her. Loved her more than he'd ever loved anything. 'Will you marry me?' he asked. 'You know how I feel about ya.'

'Oh, Smythe,' she sighed. 'How can you ask me that now? I don't know what I feel anymore. I'm so confused I don't know if I'm comin' or goin'.'

'Just think about it. That's all I'm asking.' He stood up quickly and raised his hands in a supplicating gesture. 'Don't answer right away. I know you've had a bit of a shock.'

'A bit of a shock?' she echoed. 'Is that what you call it? Let me ask you this. What if the tables were turned? What if I'd brought you out here tonight and told you something like this about me?'

'I'd try to be forgivin' and understandin',' he said quickly. He couldn't imagine Betsy telling him anything that would make him not love her.

'What if I told you I was married?' she asked. She knew exactly how to get to him.

'All right,' he said, 'I'd probably not be *that* understanding. But even if it was somethin' like that, I'd not just shut you out of my life, Betsy. I'd find a way for us to be together. Please, lass. What we've got is worth something.'

Betsy knew that was true. But her sense of anger and betrayal went deep. Deeper, perhaps, than she could make him understand. 'I need some time.'

'How much time?'

'I don't know,' she replied impatiently. 'Enough to get over the shock and try and think clearly.'

'I guess I can understand that.'

She turned and started back toward the house. Her back was poker straight, and she held her head high, refusing to give in to the awful despair that threatened to overwhelm her. She was determined to get back to the safety of her room before she broke down and started crying.

'Betsy,' he called softly. 'Are you going to tell the others?'

She stopped but didn't turn to look at him. 'That's for you to do.'

'It's a bit of a mess,' he said.

'But it's your mess, Smythe. You made it; now you clean it up.'

CHAPTER NINE

Hatchet knew he ought to be ashamed of himself, but he wasn't. Paying for information was a bit of a blow to his pride, but at his age, he'd decided his pride could stand it. In any case, one had to do what one had to do if one wanted results. Besides, he told himself, it wasn't as if madam hadn't crossed a palm with silver a time or two in the past.

He twisted slightly in his chair, vainly trying to find a more comfortable portion while he waited for his hostess to return. But the chair, like everything else in the drawing room, appeared to be on its last legs. The stuffing beneath the worn blue silk was knotted in some spots and nonexistent in others. No matter how one shifted or turned, it was dreadfully uncomfortable. The whole place was dreadfully uncomfortable, he decided.

And it smelled as well. The windows were caked with dirt and closed shut. The air was stale, with faint overtones of sour milk and mildewed cloth. Hatchet tried breathing through his mouth as he gazed curiously around the room.

The once-elegant home of the aristocratic Morlands had fallen on hard times. The delicate moldings on the high ceiling were cracked and broken in places, the gold and white striped wallpaper was faded, the chandelier was covered in cobwebs, and the thin velvet curtains were so stained with soot and grime that you had to squint to tell that they'd once been a lovely pale gold. But Hatchet wasn't one to look a gift horse in the mouth. The reason he was even sitting here at all was because he'd taken one look at the outside of the huge house and realized that the only things Lady Henrietta Morland had left were a worthless title and this mouldering pile of bricks.

If there was one thing he knew about aristocrats, it was that despite their disdain for money, when they didn't have it, they'd do anything to get it.

So he'd taken a gamble, and it appeared to have paid off.

The door creaked open and Lady Henrietta appeared. She was a tall, sparse woman with a hawk nose, deep-set watery hazel eyes and iron-gray hair pulled severely back in a topknot. She was dressed in a long-sleeved, black bombazine dress. 'Sorry to keep you waiting,' she said brusquely. 'But I had to take my medicine. Now, how much did you say your paper was willing to pay for my story?'

'Fifteen pounds, ma'am,' he replied. Silently, he prayed to whatever deity might be listening that this woman actually knew something useful. This was an exorbitant amount of cash he was going to part with, and he wanted his money's worth. 'Provided, of course, that you can verify you actually knew the victim, Miss Mirabelle Daws.'

'Don't be absurd, man,' she said curtly. 'Of course I knew her. I knew her sister as well. Met each of them the same way, coming over from Australia on the *Island Star*.'

'I wasn't impuning your honesty, ma'am,' Hatchet said quickly. 'A lady of your class and background is obviously above reproach on matters of character. But it's my editor that needs convincing,' he said conspiratorially. 'Proof, as it were. He's an American.'

'I can give you all the proof you need.' She stared at him out of hard, shrewd eyes. 'But I still don't understand why an American newspaper is interested in this murder. Don't they have enough of their own over there?'

'They do indeed, ma'am,' he agreed. 'But there is an enormous amount of interest in this particular one. It has what my editor calls "human interest."'

'Why?' Lady Henrietta walked towards a table next to the door. 'Mirabelle Daws was a nobody. Why should anyone care how she got killed?' She opened the drawer in the table and pulled out a flat, white packet. Opening the packet, she slipped out a photograph, stared at it and nodded in satisfaction.

Hatchet watched her curiously. 'I understand she was quite wealthy,' he said.

Lady Henrietta snorted and tucked the photograph into the pocket of her skirt. 'She had money, but she had no breeding. She kept house for her brother somewhere out in the outback. I believe she actually took in boarders while her brother was away working his mine.' She advanced towards him, a malicious smile on her face. 'The family were peasants, you know. Despite their mine and the property in the outback. Her sister was a lady's maid.'

'I know.' Hatchet smiled thinly. He was glad now that he'd only offered her fifteen pounds and not twenty-five. Hidebound old snob. It no longer bothered him that he'd obtained entry into this house under false pretenses. Since he'd gotten involved with the household at Upper Edmonton Gardens, his own ideas about the class system and right and wrong had completely changed. 'That's one of the reasons my newspaper is so interested in the murder. Americans like what we call rags-to-riches stories,' he explained eagerly. 'They'll be fascinated with the story of the Daws women. One of them was essentially a mail-order bride, and the other was a murder victim.'

'Mail-order bride? Humph, yes, I imagine that's what you'd call it. I call it disgusting. Annabelle Daws writes a few letters to a stupid rich Englishman and then ends up his wife. While her employer, that poor Mrs Moulton, ended up so humiliated she couldn't even face coming back to England. It's not right, I tell you.'

'What's not right?' he pressed.

'That people like that should have money,' she cried. 'Can you imagine it? Mrs Moulton, a widow from one of the finest families in the realm, had to come home to England in a tiny closet of a cabin while her maid came back in a suite. It was utterly disgusting. A lady's maid, eating at the captain's table. Both of them did, you know. These days, all it takes is money. Breeding and lineage count for nothing. But at least Annabelle Daws had the good grace to know she was among her betters and kept her mouth shut.'

'I take it Mirabelle didn't?' he asked. Hatchet had no idea if he was getting value for money, but he was certainly getting an earful and quite enjoying himself. Apparently, even thinking about the uppity Daws women was enough to make Lady Henrietta have a fit.

'She thought she was as good as the queen,' Lady Henrietta snapped. 'Had the nerve to lecture me on the value of hard work and how the decadent aristocrats had ruined the country. Can you believe it? Flounced about all over the ship, twirling those ridiculous opals and telling anyone who'd listen how she was going to England to straighten things out. Some of us tried to tell her that under English law you couldn't just waltz in and snatch an Englishman's wife, but she'd have none of it. Said English law was for fools and idiots, and she'd do whatever she had to to make sure her sister got away from that monster. It was shocking. Utterly shocking.'

'But, ma'am, even English law doesn't compel a woman to live with a husband who treats her badly,' Hatchet charged.

'She'd not get a penny of her husband's money if she left,' Lady Henrietta cried wildly. She began pacing back and forth in front of the table. 'Not one penny, and she'd not deserve it either.'

Hatchet wasn't surprised by the woman's agitated behaviour. Strange as it was, it was quite in keeping with what he was sure was her character. She was the type who felt terribly upset by anyone even daring to suggest, through word or deed, the British class system wasn't perfect. Mirabelle Daws not only questioned it; she made it abundantly clear she'd no respect for it or aristocratic leeches like the Morland woman.

'I'm surprised the captain didn't have Miss Daws moved to another table,' Hatchet said. His tone was only slightly sarcastic, but it went right past Lady Henrietta. 'It appears her presence upset you greatly.'

'Humph, I'd have thought so as well,' she replied haughtily. 'But the captain did nothing. He actually seemed to find the woman amusing. Well, he's going to regret that, I assure you. As soon as I returned, I wrote a letter to Hamilton-Dyston. They pay attention to my letters. My late husband was a shareholder in the company.'

'That must bring you in a handsome dividend,' Hatchet said. 'They do quite well in the Australian trade.' He was probing to see how a woman of her obviously limited means managed two expensive trips to Australia in the last year.

She had the good grace to look embarrassed. 'Actually, we sold the shares before my dear husband passed away. But I do get to travel on their vessels whenever I want.'

'I expect that's quite convenient for you, ma'am,' he enthused. 'Especially if you have business interests there.'

'I have family that I go to visit,' she replied. 'My cousin has a very large holding outside of Sydney.'

And Hatchet would bet his last penny that said cousin cringed every time Lady Henrietta showed up on the doorstep. 'Is there anything else you can tell me about Mirabelle Daws?' He'd not really learned anything he didn't already know.

'Only that she was an ill-bred woman who shouldn't have ever left the outback.'

'Like her sister?'

Lady Henrietta shrugged. 'Annabelle was a bit better. But then she'd learned her manners from working for the Moultons.'

'I take it you and Miss Daws were well acquainted by the time the vessel reached London. You certainly seem to know an awful lot about her.'

'I don't become "well acquainted" with persons of her sort.'

Hatchet tried to ignore the sinking feeling in the pit of his stomach. He'd learned nothing. And he was out fifteen pounds. 'I see.' He rose to his feet.

Lady Henrietta's eyes widened in alarm as she watched him get up. 'Where's my money?'

He started to reach his coat and then hesitated. 'Uh, I say, this is awkward, but I do need some proof that you did actually know the victim.' He fully intended to fulfil his end of the bargain, but he might as well get something tangible for his fifteen quid.

She reached into her pocket and took out the photograph. 'This was taken on board the *Island Star*,' she handed it to him. 'The woman standing next to me was Mrs Moulton. The person just to her right is Annabelle Daws. Is that proof enough for you?'

'I'd rather have a photograph of Mirabelle Daws.'

'I don't have one of her. But you said you wanted proof I knew the Daws women. Well, this is a picture of Annabelle Daws.'

'I suppose it'll do,' he said. 'Though a photograph of the murder victim would have been better.' He pulled out several bills.

She stepped back. 'Put them on the tray by the door,' she instructed.

'As you wish, ma'am.' He tucked the photograph in his pocket. 'Thank you for seeing me. I'll be on my way now.' He gave her a quick, barely perceptible head bob. Not because he had any genuine respect for her, but because it would be suspicious if he stopped playing his part now. That of an English gentleman forced to do something distasteful to make a living.

'I'll ring for Collins to see you out,' she said, yanking on the frayed bellpull that dangled forlornly next to the door.

'There's no need,' he protested. He rather suspected she'd only done it to make sure he didn't scarper without putting down the cash. 'I can see myself out. Please don't trouble your staff.'

'That's what he's here for,' she replied arrogantly. 'What did you say your name was again?'

Hatchet was ready for that question. 'It was Puffy, ma'am. Rollo Puffy.'

Wiggins thought his day couldn't get any worse. First, Smythe was as grouchy as a dog with a sore paw, Betsy was barely speakin' to anyone, Mrs Goodge had caught him snatchin' one of her special sticky buns, and even Mrs Jeffries was so preoccupied that she'd probably not heard a word he'd said when he'd left this morning.

And now this. He stared miserably at the young girl

hurrying toward Charing Cross. He didn't know what to do. She was the tweeny he'd met that first day, the one he was sure knew more than she was telling. He'd popped along to Sheridan Square right early today and hit a spot of luck. He'd seen her sweepin' the front door stoop. Mind you, when he'd tried to talk to her, she'd not been real friendly. But he had learned that the funeral for that poor Miss Daws was tomorrow morning and that no one excepting the family was invited. Then she'd dropped the real news. She was leavin' that day. Taking the midday train home to her people and never setting foot in London again.

He'd tried to keep her talking, but he'd failed. Then Mrs Prosper had come out and spoken to the girl. Wiggins couldn't hear much of what was said, just saw Fiona nod her head up and down a few times and then she'd said, "Yes, Mrs Prosper," curtsied and hurried back inside.

Wiggins refused to give up. He knew this girl knew something. He'd hovered for hours waiting for her to come out. And it hadn't been easy either. The murder had made the residents of Sheridan Square nervous. Several people had come out and asked him his business. Luckily, the use of Inspector Witherspoon's name had worked like magic. Now he hoped that he wouldn't be in even more hot water when he got home. What if someone complained to the inspector?

The girl darted into the station. Considering that she was carrying a large carpetbag, she moved fairly quickly. Wiggins rushed after her. Just inside the huge door, he skidded to a halt. She was at the ticket counter. Directly above where she stood, there was a large

How'd you get in to see this woman?' Luty
[de]manded.

Hatchet smiled broadly. 'That was easy. I pre-
[ten]ded to be an American newspaper reporter doing
[a s]tory on Mirabelle Daws. I used the name Rollo
[Pu]ffy. That way, if Lady Henrietta said anything to
[In]spector Witherspoon, it would be the same name as
[M]adam so cleverly used when she sent the telegram.'

'Touché, Hatchet.' Luty laughed.

'Who's Rollo Puffy?' Betsy asked. She put the pho-
[t]ograph down next to her teacup.

'I'll tell you later,' Luty promised, 'after the men
leave for the pub tonight.'

'Is that it, Hatchet?' Mrs Jeffries asked quickly.

'I'm afraid so, ma'am,' he admitted. He noticed
that his photograph wasn't eliciting much interest.
No one else even bothered to pick it up. He started to
reach for it, fully intending to stuff it back in his coat
pocket, when he was distracted by Wiggins.

'I've got something to say,' the footman said eagerly.
'I finally had a word with Fiona today. Caught her at
the train station as she was fixin' to leave town.'

'Who's Fiona?' Smythe asked.

'You remember, she were that tweeny I told ya
about that first day,' Wiggins said. 'The one who I
thought was hidin' something. I were right, she was
hidin' somethin'. That's one of the reasons she's leavin'
town. Scared, she is. Right scared that's she's goin' to
be next.'

Everyone leaned forward eagerly.

Wiggins, seeing that he now had their full attention, paused and reached for his tea.

clack board showing departure and arrival times.
Wiggins smiled. There wasn't a train leaving for at
least twenty minutes. Sighing in relief, he relaxed. At
least she wasn't rushing off right this minute. Maybe
now that she was away from the Prosper house, she'd
not be so unfriendly.

He leaned against the wall and watched her. In a
few moments, she had her ticket. Then she picked up
the carpetbag and started for the platform.

Wiggins was relieved about that as well. He'd been
worried she might head for the ladies' waiting room.
He kept a close eye on her as she moved out into
the cavernous station, and when he was sure he could
follow her safely, he went after her.

'Are you sure we can't be seen from here?' the inspector asked for the third time. He and Barnes were
standing behind a covered doorway in a warehouse
across the street from the Sailor's Whistle. The pub
was small and had a tiny window on each side of the
door. It was crammed in between a derelict office
building on one side and a cluttered wharf on the
other.

'Absolutely, sir.' He patted the wood that covered
half of the recessed doorway. 'We've had a bit of luck.
They're goin' to be tearin' this place down in a couple
of months. That's why they started boarding things
up, sir. Wanted to make sure no one got in and took
root.'

'Yes,' Witherspoon mused. 'I suppose we have had
our share of good fortune. You're absolutely certain
there isn't any other way in or out of the pub?'

'Absolutely, sir,' Barnes said patiently. 'They used to have a bit of a wharf so that boats could pull up and let people in and out. But it rotted years ago, and they boarded over the back door. Take my word for it, sir. Whoever is fencing that necklace has to come in through the front door. Right under our noses as it were.'

'Good.' Witherspoon walked back out into the street. Barnes was right on his heels. 'Then we'll be back this evening. If we hurry, we ought to have enough time to get a bite to eat. It might be quite a long night. We've no idea what time the woman might be showing up. How many lads are we leaving to watch the place?'

'Three, sir,' Barnes replied. 'None of them in uniform either. They're good coppers, sir. They'll not be spotted. Two of them are from around this area. They're the ones I'm puttin' on the inside tonight. Tonight, of course, we'll have several more on hand in case we have to make an arrest.'

Mrs Jeffries wasn't in a particularly good mood herself, so when she saw Betsy's long face and Smythe's tight-lipped expression, she knew this meeting might not run smoothly.

'Let's get this done, then,' Mrs Goodge ordered as she placed the tea tray on the table 'I've got more people coming through here in an hour or two, and I'll need this kitchen clear if I'm to get information out of anyone.'

Her tone was a tad testy, a sure sign that she'd not learned anything useful either.

'I agree,' Mrs Jeffries said. 'Quickly, [...] your seats.' For a few moments the only [...] the scraping of chairs and the swish o[...] people took their places around the table[...] one has anything to report . . .'

'I've got something to report,' Hatchet s[...] It wasn't much, but at least he'd come [...] something. 'I tracked down Lady Henrietta [...] he continued. 'She was on the same ship as [...] Daws. She was also on the same vessel as A[...] Daws Prosper. She knew both women.'

'How very interesting,' Mrs Jeffries said. She [...]ced herself to be patient. Though what she was most interested in doing at this meeting was making their plans for this evening's hunt at the Sailor's Whistle pub. She fully intended that someone from this household would witness everything that went on. 'Did you learn anything new?'

Hatchet opened his mouth to reply and then clamped it shut again and slumped in his chair. 'No[...] really. I simply got confirmation of what Judit[...] Brinkman reported. Mirabelle Daws wasn't shy wit[...] expressing her opinion to all and sundry. But I did ge[...] a photograph,' he reached in his pocket, pulled it ou[...] and tossed it onto the tabletop. 'Unfortunately, it's n[...] one of Mirabelle Daws.'

'Who is it, then?' Betsy asked as she picked it up.

'Lady Henrietta and Annabelle Prosper,' [...] replied. 'Lady Henrietta's on the right, the woma[...] next to her is that Mrs Moulton. Annabelle Daws [...] standing a few feet back. She's the one in the da[...] shawl.'

'Get on with it, Wiggins,' Mrs Goodge ordered. 'We've not got all night. Not only do I have my sources comin' in, but we've got to make some plans for this evening.'

'I'm gettin' to it,' he complained. Why was he always the one that got rushed? 'Anyways, I saw Fiona outside the Prosper 'ouse, but I didn't get a chance to speak to 'er. Finally caught up with her at the railway station. At first, she weren't too friendly.' He didn't tell them about her threatenin' to call the police on him when he'd first showed up. 'But after we'd talked for a few minutes, she were willin' to tell me a few things.' Again, he'd used the inspector's name. That and a cup of tea had calmed the girl considerably. 'She was right nervous. Claimed that Mrs Prosper were pretendin' she didn't want the girl to go because of the funeral bein' tomorrow.'

'That's understandable,' Mrs Goodge put in. 'A funeral reception takes a lot of work. They'll have a lot of people to cater for.'

'But they'll not,' Wiggins argued. 'That's one of the reasons Fiona left. She thinks the whole bunch of 'em is actin' right strange. No one's goin' to the funeral but the immediate family. There's to be no reception at all. They're not even letting some of the people from the ship come. The purser sent his condolences and asked when the service would be, and Mrs Prosper sent him a nasty note sayin' he shouldn't come, that it was to be family only. That Judith Brinkman wanted to come as well, and the Prospers did the same thing to her. Fiona says the whole thing gives her a funny feelin'.'

'Why would the Prospers' lack of a funeral reception make the tweeny leave?' Betsy asked. 'A private funeral isn't that unusual, especially as Mirabelle Daws didn't really know anyone here.'

'It weren't just that,' Wiggins continued. 'It were a lot of things that scared Fiona. It seems that on the night of the murder, Fiona heard half the household up and down and out and about. Her room is just over the second floor, right over the family bedrooms. Well, Fiona couldn't sleep that night 'cause Sally, that's the girl she shares with, was snorin' somethin' awful. About half past four, she was wide awake and worryin' that she'd be dead tired the next day. All of a sudden, she hears the bedroom door below her creakin' open. Then she heard footsteps crossing the landing and going down the front stairs::

'Did she get up and see who it was?'

He shook his head. 'No, she thought at the time that she knew who it was. She thought it was Mrs Prosper sneakin' out to the garden to meet Mr Heckston.'

'Blimey, I guess everyone did know about those two,' Smythe muttered softly.

'But it weren't Mrs Prosper,' Wiggins explained, 'because fifteen or so minutes later, she heard another door open. This time, she did stick her head out to see what was goin' on. Well, blow me for a game of tin soldiers if she didn't get the surprise of her life.'

'Who was it?' Betsy demanded.

'Eldon Prosper. That's who it was. Standing in the hallway big as life.' Wiggins beamed proudly. 'That's why she left town. She got up the next morning and mentioned Mr Prosper's name to the housekeeper

192

only to be told that he'd not come back from Edin-burg. Then she found out about the murder. She claimed she tried to talk to Mrs Prosper's maid about everything, about how she didn't like what was goin' on, but the maid refused to listen. But then Fiona says the woman drinks.'

'She does,' Betsy agreed.

'How'd you know?' Smythe asked sharply.

'I smelled it on her breath when we talked,' Betsy said.

'Can I finish?' Wiggins asked. 'Poor Fiona is in a right old state. Something funny were goin' on, and she'd no idea what.'

'Who does she think did it?' Mrs Goodge asked.

'She's no idea.' Wiggins shrugged. 'But consid-erin' how much comin' and goin' there was from that house that night, she thought it best to leave.'

No one said anything for a moment. Finally, Mrs Jeffries said, 'That's very interesting, Wiggins. You've done very well. I'm just wondering if we ought to find a way to get this information to the inspector.'

'Why don't we hold off on that, Mrs J?' Smythe suggested. 'Let's see what 'appens at the Sailor's Whis-tle tonight.'

'That's probably a good idea,' she replied. 'If needed, we can always make sure the inspector knows the girl left the household suddenly. That alone would be cause enough for him to question her.' She looked at Wiggins. 'Why didn't she tell the police any of this when she was questioned before? Inspector Wither-spoon always makes sure he talks to everyone.'

Wiggins had asked the girl the same question. 'She

weren't questioned by our inspector. One of the uniformed lads did it. She said that she was afraid to say too much because both Mrs Prosper and Mrs McCabe kept hanging about the kitchen when the policeman was talking to 'er.'

Mrs Jeffries frowned in disapproval but said nothing. She'd thought the inspector went to great lengths to insure that everyone was questioned privately. Apparently, his standards were slipping a bit.

'But what does it mean?' Luty asked. 'Like the boy says, there was so much comin' and goin' that night, it's nigh on impossible to tell who mighta done the killin'.'

'Who had the motive?' Mrs Goodge added. 'Seems to me that's where we ought to really start.'

'Eldon Prosper, for one,' Smythe said softly. 'He was afraid Mirabelle would talk his wife into going back to Australia. That's a powerful motive for some men, the idea of losin' someone they love.' He glanced at Betsy as he spoke. And this time she didn't look away.

'That Mrs McCabe had a motive as well,' Mrs Goodge argued. 'I think hers is even stronger. If Mrs Prosper left, she'd be stuck home with her brother for the rest of her life, and we know she wanted to go off traveling with her friend.'

'It seems to me that the only person who didn't have a motive is Mrs Prosper,' Hatchet commented.

'Perhaps she did,' Mrs Jeffries said. 'Perhaps she didn't want her wanton behaviour with her neighbor, Mr Heckston, getting back to her brother in Australia. After all, we know nothing of the brother. Perhaps if he knew Mrs Prosper had been unfaithful to her marriage vows, he'd cut her off completely.'

'But why should she care?' Betsy pointed out. 'She knows her husband is so besotted with her that he'll not turn her out into the streets. He's rich as well. I don't think she'd murder her own sister on the off chance that the sister might spill the beans to a brother that's halfway 'round the world. Besides, from what we know of Mirabelle, I think there's a good chance her brother is much the same. He probably wouldn't care what Annabelle Prosper had been up to with her neighbor.'

'You've got a point.' Mrs Jeffries nodded slowly. There were so many unexplained questions. So much that she didn't understand. But right now, there wasn't time to think about them. They had to decide how they were going to keep watch on the pub. Inspector Witherspoon might be doing quite well on this case, but she and the others weren't quite ready to give up. 'If no one else has anything to add, perhaps we'd better discuss how we're going to deal with tonight's problem.'

'I think Hatchet, Wiggins and I ought to nip out and keep an eye on the Sailor's Whistle. We can see who shows up to sell that necklace.'

'Don't you mean you can see who the killer is?' Mrs Goodge groused. She was annoyed that so far, she'd not added one useful clue to this investigation.

'We don't know that the person with the necklace is the murderer,' Mrs Jeffries insisted as she remembered the inspector's comment to Nivens. But even as the words left her lips, they had a hollow ring. The

195

truth was, whoever showed up with the jewels probably had killed Mirabelle Daws. And the inspector had essentially come to that point without much help from any of them. It was depressing, but she refused to give in to it.

She glanced at Smythe and Betsy. She could tell by the way they occasionally smiled at each other that the ice between them was melting. She was fairly certain that there would be a big change coming from that direction. The idea didn't really displease her. It might make life a bit more interesting if those two came to their senses and realized they cared deeply for one another. Besides, she thought, even if they did get engaged or even married, that didn't mean their investigations would end. Betsy and Smythe loved snooping too much.

'We don't know that the person fencing the jewels ain't the killer either,' Smythe pointed out. He got up. 'There's a warehouse right across the street from the pub where we can see everything.'

'Won't the police be using it?' Mrs Jeffries asked.

'Probably.' Smythe shrugged. 'But they'll be on the ground floor. I've got us a way into the second floor. There's a right nice view from the window up there.'

CHAPTER TEN

'The inspector is doin' quite well on his own this time, isn't he?' Mrs Goodge commented as soon as the men had left.

'Indeed he is,' Mrs Jeffries agreed. 'But that's no reason for us not to do our best.'

The cook didn't look convinced. 'I suppose you're right,' she replied slowly. 'But I can't help thinkin' that I've wasted an awful lot of food in the past couple of days. I've not found out anything useful.'

'Now don't be so down in the mouth,' Luty chided. 'We won't know what's useful and what's not until after we catch the killer. Besides, just because we ain't had much luck gettin' the jump on the inspector so far don't mean we ain't contributin'. Think of poor Hatchet. Drags his old bones all the way out to Colchester to see that Lady Henrietta, and he don't find out anything more than what we already know. But he didn't let that get him down none. He went ahead and went out tonight with the others. It's just like Hepzibah says; we don't know that the case is over just because the inspector is fixin' to grab some woman tryin' to sell a necklace. Besides, maybe no one will show at all tonight.'

'Well said, Luty,' the housekeeper commented. 'By the way, now that Hatchet is gone, will you please tell us something? Who is Rollo Puffy?'

Luty laughed. 'He was, or for all I know, still is, one of the best con men operating in the United States. He took Hatchet and a few others real good.'

'What do you mean?' Betsy asked curiously. 'Took him how?'

'For money,' Luty replied. 'Rollo Puffy cost poor old Hatchet three thousand dollars. Mind you, it was a number of years back, before we came to London. Hatchet had just come to work for me. My husband was still alive back in those days, and we had us a big house up on Nob Hill. Well, Hatchet had somehow met up with this real nice old feller named Rollo Puffy. Puffy claimed that he'd made a fortune in the lumber business up in the northwest and had come to San Francisco to sell this big, fancy yacht.' She reached for the pot and poured herself more tea. 'Anyway, Hatchet come in one evening sayin' that Puffy wanted to get shut of this yacht so danged bad, he was goin' to sell it real cheap. Puffy said he was goin' to buy an even bigger one and sail it back to Seattle. He didn't need two boats. Now the reason Hatchet told me and my husband about it was because we'd invested some of his money for him. We both thought it sounded fishy, but we didn't like to say nothin'. So we all got in the carriage and went down to the dock to have a look at the yacht.' She smiled and shook her head at the memory. 'It was a beauty. Over forty foot long and with the prettiest white and gold trim you ever saw. To make a long story short, Hatchet gave Puffy the money that night. Even though we thought the boat were pretty, we were against him doin' it. Just didn't stand to reason that even a rich man would sell something that valuable for three thousand dollars. But it was Hatchet's money, and he did as he wanted. He told us he was goin' to set sail for the Pacific islands. Give up butlerin' and see something of the world. But things didn't work out like that.'

'What happened?' Mrs Goodge asked eagerly.

'When he went back to the dock the next morning, the yacht was nowhere to be seen. But there were three other people there, and they was all madder than spit.'

'I take it the man had sold the yacht to these three as well,' Mrs Jeffries said.

'Absolutely. And the reason the feller worked the scam so easy was that there really was a Rollo Puffy, and he really was an eccentric millionaire. He kept a huge suite at one of the fanciest hotels in town and had a letter of credit deposited at the Bank of California. This feller claimin' to be Puffy had moved into his suite at the Fremont Hotel and from the gossip I got later, even though the bank did try to hush it up, he'd used the line of credit too.'

'But how did this man get away with pretending to be someone he wasn't?' Betsy asked.

'Easy.' Luty grinned and put down her cup. 'No one had ever seen Puffy. He was rich as sin, but he never came to town. Lots of fellows like him back in those days. Fellows that struck it rich back in the 1840s and

50s and didn't know what to do with all that money. Puffy had deposited the letter of credit and rented the rooms at the Fremont through an agent. But the agent was long gone by the time the sharpster come around pretendin' to be Puffy.'

'Poor Hatchet,' Mrs Jeffries said sympathetically. 'That must have been quite a blow to him. Losing all that money.'

'It hurt his pride worse than his pocketbook,' Luty replied. 'But I didn't use Puffy's name on that telegram just to niggle at Hatchet. I used it because it's probably the last name on earth that'll ever be heard tell here in England. The last thing I'd ever want to do is make up a name and have some poor soul have to suffer for what we done.'

'Did you hear something, sir?' Barnes asked Witherspoon. He stuck his head around the wooden partition and stared hard up and down the street. 'I thought I heard a thumping noise.'

'I expect it's just the sound of the bumpers hitting against the wharf,' Witherspoon replied. He'd not heard anything.

'It sounded closer than that, sir. Almost like it was right over our heads.'

'There's nothing over our heads, Constable. No one's been in this building for ages,' Witherspoon said. 'I expect there's so much rot upstairs that it wouldn't be safe to walk across the floor. Do you see anything yet?'

'Not yet, sir.' Barnes stuck his head back in. He wasn't concerned that they would be spotted. To begin with, there wasn't anyone about, and secondly they were well hidden. 'But he ought to be here soon. Accordin' to what Nivens's people told us, Jon McGee is back in town. He holds court here every night from eight o'clock on.'

'Hmmm . . yes. But it's almost eight, and we've not seen anyone go in except a few locals and our own lads. I don't think this McGee fellow could have slipped past us either, not from the description we got from the lads in K division.'

'He'll be along soon, sir. And the minute he shows, we'll spot him. There's not too many peg-legged crooks working this part of London.' Suddenly, Barnes cocked his ear toward the road and then stuck his head back out.

'Someone's comin' now, sir.' He paused for a brief second. 'It's him, sir. It's McGee. He and one of his mates are just coming past the wharf.'

Witherspoon stuck his head out as well. Holding his breath, he watched the two men, one with a wooden peg leg, make their way toward the door of the Sailor's Whistle. 'Excellent. Now all we have to do is wait for the lady to arrive, and we'll be right as rain.'

'You're convinced that whoever shows up with the necklace is our killer, sir?' Barnes asked.

'Probably,' the inspector replied. 'But we'll have to see what happens, won't we? I don't want to make too many assumptions about tonight. I shouldn't like to arrest the wrong person.' The inspector had a horror about that. He had a great deal of faith in the British justice system. But in a murder case where the penalty was probably going to be death, he wanted to make absolutely sure that for his part, he arrested the guilty party.

Witherspoon would rather see the guilty go free than an innocent person hang.

'Be quiet,' Smythe hissed at Wiggins. 'You keep thumping about like that, the inspector or one of his lads will be up here to see what's goin' on.'

'I'm not movin' on purpose,' Wiggins gave himself another hard shake and smacked at the air in front of him. 'There's a spider on me somewhere.'

'There's nothing on you,' Hatchet soothed.

'Yes, there is.' Wiggins jiggled up and down on the balls of his feet. 'I walked through its ruddy web.'

'Stop that or I'll box yer ears,' Smythe whispered. 'These floorboards are old as sin and creakin' like an old woman's bones.'

'But the inspector and Constable Barnes is outside the building,' Wiggins protested. 'They can't 'ear nuthin'.' But he did force himself to stand still. He slapped his hand to his neck, thinking he felt a tickle on his skin.

'Can you see, Smythe?' Hatchet asked. They'd wiped a fairly large amount of grime off the window. But the night was dark, and his eyes weren't as sharp as they used to be.

'The view's just fine. I think that's Jon McGee and one of his thugs goin' in now.' He raised his hand and wiped at his cheek. This place was so filthy that even standing in it made you feel dirty. The very air itself reeked of grime and grit. It also reeked of lots of other things, most of them nasty. The river being so close didn't help much. In this part of town the water mainly smelled of rancid vegetation and rotting fish. 'Stinks, doesn't it?' he commented idly.

'It shouldn't be for much longer,' Hatchet replied. 'Not if our lady wants to be home at a reasonable hour.'

'Ouch.' Wiggins slapped himself on the cheek, again thinking he'd felt something scuttling across his face.

'Let's just 'ope she doesn't change her mind on us,' the coachman muttered.

From a distance, they heard the sound of a carriage turning into the street.

'That sounds like a cab,' Smythe said, 'and if it is, it's proably her. In this neighborhood, there ain't much carriage trade after dark.'

Witherspoon's whole body stiffened as he watched the cab pull up on the narrow street in front of the pub. A heavily veiled woman stepped out. Despite the warmth of the summer evening, she carried a large fur muff. She handed the driver some coins, and they heard her murmur something to him. But her tone was too low for them to understand what she said.

'Right, ma'am,' the driver replied. 'I'll be back for you in fifteen minutes and not a moment later.' He cracked the whip in the air and moved off.

The woman stood in front of the door and paused, probably to gather her courage, and went inside.

Witherspoon and Barnes didn't take their eyes off the door. 'I think it's her, sir,' the constable muttered.

'We'll know in a moment.' Just as the words left Witherspoon's mouth, the door opened and a young man dressed in workingman's clothes stepped out. He looked straight at the two policemen and shook his head. Then he went back inside.

'It's her,' Witherspoon said in relief. He really wanted this case finished. Even if this person wasn't the killer, at least apprehending her would bring them one step closer to solving the murder. He hoped.

The minutes ticked by. It got so quiet that they could hear the sound of the water lapping against the dilapidated wharf. Finally, after what seemed hours but was really only ten minutes or so, the door opened. Jon McGee and the veiled woman both stepped outside.

McGee took the woman's elbow, and they walked away from the pub, toward the wharf. Toward the darkness.

'Drat,' Witherspoon murmured. 'Now he's moved out of the light.'

'I think that was the idea,' Barnes said softly. He didn't like this. Didn't like it one bit. The constable held his breath as he watched the fence edging the woman further and further away from them.

McGee finally stopped. The two of them were now a good fifty feet off and standing in an area that was considerably darker than the spot outside the pub.

But there was still enough light to make out what few details Barnes discovered, as he watched McGee reach into his coat pocket and pull out a small packet. He extended it towards the woman. She reached for it, but he jerked back, keeping the packet just out of reach. 'I'll have the other first,' he told her.

Witherspoon nodded in satisfaction, glad that they could hear what was being said. McGee apparently felt so safe here that he didn't bother to lower his voice.

The woman said nothing; she merely reached into her muff and drew out a cloth bag. They made the exchange.

McGee started to open the bag. Barnes and Witherspoon stepped out into the street, and the constable blew long and hard on the whistle he'd had at the ready.

Policemen poured out into the street. The three in plain clothes rushed out of the pub, two more that had been hiding behind a pile of rubbish on the wharf leapt out, and three others came flying from around the corner.

McGee realized what was happening first. He spotted Barnes and Witherspoon closing in quickly. Grabbing the woman, he hurled her towards the two policemen and made a mad dash in the other direction, his wooden leg thumping wildly as he ran.

The woman gave an inelegant squawk as she flew through the air and slapped into Witherspoon. He managed to catch her around the waist and by throwing all his body weight forward, he kept them from hitting the pavement.

Barnes and three other policemen went flying after McGee. The fence bolted towards the intersection, watching over his shoulder as he ran. The constable saw what was happening first and shouted a warning at McGee, but to no avail. The fence went hurtling straight into the hansom cab that had just pulled around the corner.

The cabbie pulled hard on the reins, but there simply wasn't time to stop. McGee was lucky, though. Instead of actually being trampled, he was butted in the stomach by the panicked horse and sent flying. He landed a couple of feet away from two police constables. Moaning, he tried to get up, couldn't, and collapsed back onto the pavement.

'See about him, Barnes,' Witherspoon yelled as he struggled to hold onto the woman. By now, she was pulling, pushing, shoving and doing all manner of unladylike things to get free of the inspector's grasp. But he held firm.

Two police constables leapt into the fray. Within a few moments, they had their quarry firmly, each one grasping one of the woman's arms. Witherspoon, adjusting his glasses, stepped back and surveyed the scene.

Barnes knelt down next to McGee, reached into the groaning man's coat pocket and took out the soft cloth bag. He opened the bag, reached in, and pulled out a long necklace. 'I think this is it, sir,' he called.

'I don't know how that got in my pocket,' McGee argued. 'That tart must have planted it on me.'

'Is he going to be all right?' Witherspoon asked.

'He'll be fine, sir. I don't think he's even got any broken bones.'

'Fat lot you know,' McGee snapped. He rubbed his head. 'This is a setup, this is. I'm an innocent businessman doing a bit o' legitamate business, and all of a sudden I'm set upon by coppers. It's your fault I run into that bleedin' hansom,' he accused Barnes. 'You'll be hearin' from my solicitor, you will.'

'I didn't see him coming,' cried the hansom driver. He'd stopped a few feet away and was staring open-mouthed at the scene. 'Oh my God, I've run over a cripple.'

McGee's head shot up off the pavement. 'Bugger off,' he yelled at the hapless hansom driver. 'I ain't no cripple, and if I wasn't layin' here surrounded by coppers, I'd get up and kick yer bloomin' arse all the way to Brighton.'

The cab driver ignored him. 'It wasn't my fault,' he repeated as he looked at Barnes. 'I couldn't stop. He come out of nowhere, he did. Ran smack into me.'

'You'll be hearin' from my solicitor too,' McGee screamed, incensed that the driver ignored his threats.

'Of course you couldn't stop,' Barnes assured the driver. Then he looked down at McGee. 'Save it for the judge,' he said to him. He rose to his feet and signaled for two uniformed men to take over. Then he hurried back to the inspector.

He handed Witherspoon the necklace. 'Looks like opals and diamonds to me, sir.'

The inspector held them up. Even with just the faint light from the small pub windows, the stones separating the opals glittered in the night. 'Indeed they do.' He dropped the necklace back into the bag. Then he handed it back to Barnes. 'We'll need this signed in as evidence. Now, let's see who we have here.'

The woman, still standing between the two

constables, said nothing. The inspector reached over and lifted her veil. He sighed as he stared into the frightened eyes of Marlena McCabe. 'Mrs McCabe,' he said firmly. 'You're under arrest for the murder of Mirabelle Daws.'

Marlena McCabe didn't seem to grasp that she was under arrest for murder. 'I tell you, I want to go home. My brother will be very worried about me.'

Witherspoon sighed inwardly. His suspect was sitting quite calmly in the straight-backed chair on the other side of his desk. Constable Barnes was sitting to one side as was the young police constable who was taking down the woman's statement. Not that she'd said anything particularly useful yet.

He tried again. 'Mrs McCabe, you don't seem to understand how serious your predicament is. I must advise you that you're under arrest for murder. Do you understand?'

She continued to stare at him blankly, then all of a sudden, she seemed to realize that she was at a police station and that she was in serious straits. She shuddered, and her eyes filled with tears. 'Dear God, this can't be happening.'

Finally, he thought. 'But I assure you, ma'am, it is happening. Now, we have some questions for you. How did you come to be in possession of Mirabelle Daws's necklace?' They'd not established that the necklace actually belonged to the victim as yet, but they weren't in court at the moment and consequently, he wasn't bound by the judge's rules. It was perfectly reasonable to make the assumption that the necklace did belong to the victim.

'I don't have to talk to you,' she insisted. 'I don't have to say anything.'

'That's true,' Witherspoon replied. 'You're well within your rights to call for your solicitor. However,' he leaned forward, his expression deadly serious, 'if you are innocent, you're playing right into the real murderer's hands by not telling us everything you know.'

The inspector had no idea what prompted him to say such a thing. He'd opened his mouth, and it had just popped out. Gracious, he didn't want Mrs McCabe to think she wasn't under arrest. But before he could tell her that, she started to speak.

'She was already dead when I got there,' she blurted. 'I'll admit that I took the necklace, but I didn't kill her.'

'What time did you arrive?' Barnes asked quickly.

She bit her lip. 'It was about five, I think. I'm not absolutely sure.'

'How did you know that Mirabelle Daws was in the garden?' Witherspoon asked.

'I didn't,' she replied. She looked down at the floor. 'It was only an accident that I happened to come upon her body. I'd gone out to the garden because I couldn't sleep.'

Witherspoon knew she was lying.

'That's quite a coincidence, isn't it ma'am?' Barnes said softly.

'Coincidences happen,' she said. She didn't look up from the floor. 'Can I go home now? I really would like to have few hours to rest. Tomorrow is the funeral, you know. Even though it's just going to be family, I do want to look my best.'

'No, ma'am,' the inspector said, 'I'm afraid you can't. Why didn't you call for help when you found the woman dead?'

'I don't know. I expect I ought to have called for the police. But I wasn't thinking properly.' She looked up; her face wore a dazed, panicked expression. 'I didn't wish to be involved. It is rather a shock, you know. Finding a body.'

'If you were in such a state, ma'am,' Witherspoon pressed, 'then how was it that you had the presence of mind to take the necklace?'

She said nothing for a moment. 'I know what you're trying to do. You're trying to make it look like I killed her. But I didn't. I didn't, I tell you.'

Wearily Witherspoon shook his head. He glanced over at Barnes, who nodded. They had no other course of action. 'Mrs McCabe. We're going to send a message to your brother . . .'

'No, don't,' she cried. 'There's no need to drag Eldon into this. Please, can't you just let me go home?'

'You don't understand, ma'am,' Barnes said gently. 'You're not going home. You're under arrest. We thought you'd want your family to know where you were so they could get you some legal help.'

She cocked her head to one side and stared at him. She looked utterly stunned, as though she couldn't believe what was happening. 'Does that mean you're going to put me in prison?'

Witherspoon hated this part. 'Yes, ma'am, I'm rather afraid it does.'

'Marlena McCabe!' Mrs Goodge snorted in disgust. 'I'd have never thought it was her.'

'Why not?' Betsy demanded. 'She had a motive. She didn't want her sister-in-law going home to Australia.'

'That's a pretty pathetic motive if ya ask me,' Luty put in. 'Killin' someone just so's ya don't get stuck takin' care of your kinfolk. If she'da had any gumption, she'da told her brother she was leavin' with or without his stupid allowance.'

'I must admit, I'm rather surprised,' Mrs Jeffries mused. 'Ya coulda knocked us over with a feather, too,' Wiggins said.

'I've no idea why we were all so surprised,' Hatchet added, 'it's not as though there are a huge number of female suspects in this case. But when the inspector lifted that veil, we were all very taken aback.'

No one said anything for a moment. Everyone was too busy thinking about this evening's events. Mrs Goodge finally broke the silence. 'I suppose that's it then, it's over. The inspector did it without much help from us, and that's a fact.' She looked at the housekeeper. 'You've not passed on much of what we learned, have you?'

'Not really,' Mrs Jeffries admitted. 'This time it didn't appear as if the inspector needed our assistance. He was almost always a step or two ahead of us.'

Hatchet yawned. 'Oh, I do beg your pardon.' He apologized as he realized everyone was looking at him. 'If there's nothing else, I suppose the madam and I ought to be getting home. It is very late.'

Mrs Jeffries smiled wearily. It was late. They were all tired and the case, for all intents and purposes, was probably solved. Then why did it feel so wrong? Why wasn't she secure in her own mind that justice would be done? 'We're all very tired.'

Wiggins suddenly stood up. 'You're all goin' to think I'm addled, but there's something I've got to say. I don't think it's 'er. I don't think she killed that woman. There's somethin' 'ere that's not right.'

'You only think that 'cause you don't want to admit we've not been much help on this one,' Mrs Goodge said briskly. She got up. 'I'm going to bed. I suggest the rest of you do the same.'

'We'd best be off too,' Luty said.

Smythe and Betsy said their goodnights as well and within just a few moments, it was only Wiggins and Mrs Jeffries left in the kitchen.

Mrs Jeffries noticed the forgotten photograph. 'Oh dear, Hatchet has forgotten this,' she said, picking it up.

'I'll take it round to 'im tomorrow,' Wiggins said glumly. ''Ere, give it to me.'

She smiled at the footman and handed him the photograph. She knew just how he felt. 'Wiggins, we can't always be right.'

'I know, Mrs Jeffries,' he replied. 'But there's somethin' funny 'ere. You feel it too. I could see it in yer face when we was all talkin'.' He glanced at the picture in his hand. 'But maybe I'm only seein' what I want to see.'

'Perhaps so,' she agreed. But that wasn't true. She did think there was something wrong. But before she gave Wiggins any false hope about the matter, she wanted to think about the case in the privacy of her room.

'Oh, well, best move on to other things.' He lifted the picture up and looked at it. 'Ever since Smythe and Betsy took me to that photography exhibition at the Crystal Palace, I've been right interested.'

'I agree. It is best to move on to other things.' She was delighted he was so easily diverted. She didn't want him brooding over the case all night.

Wiggins had a nice, long look. 'Who did Hatchet say this was?'

Mrs Jeffries leaned over and pointed to the two women in the foreground. 'The older one is Lady Henrietta Morland, the woman next to her is Mrs Moulton, and the one in the dark shawl in the background is Annabelle Prosper. Strange, isn't it, how life works out. I'll bet that Mrs Moulton never thought her maid would end up paying for her passage back to England.'

Wiggins continued to stare at the photograph, his expression puzzled. 'Hatchet must have got it wrong,' he finally said.

'Got what wrong?'

'Who the women are.'

'What do you mean?' Mrs Jeffries asked. But her heart had begun to beat faster, and her spirits were picking up by the seconds.

Wiggins pointed to the figure in the black shawl. 'That's not Annabelle Prosper,' he declared. 'I saw

Mrs Prosper just today. When she come out of the house to give poor Fiona a talkin' to. That's not her.' Then he pointed to the woman standing next to Lady Henrietta Morland. 'This one is.'

CHAPTER ELEVEN

'Are you sure?' Mrs Jeffries wanted to be absolutely certain the lad wasn't making a mistake. 'Both the women in the photograph are of the same height and build.'

'I'm sure as I'm standin' 'ere talkin' to you. I got a good look at Mrs Prosper when she come out of the 'ouse to have a natter at poor Fiona. That's 'er, all right,' he insisted, pointing to the likeness of Abigail Moulton. 'So Hatchet musta got it wrong. I tell ya, Mrs J, I knew there were something right funny about this whole case. I knew it. I could feel it in my bones, so to speak.'

But Mrs Jeffries wasn't listening. She was thinking furiously. Was it possible? Could it be that once again, they'd made a grave error in their whole approach to this case? If what she suspected was true, then it explained so very much. They'd been concentrating on the wrong question all along. They should have been asking 'why' Mirabelle Daws, a woman who'd never set foot in England before, had been murdered. Instead, they'd been concentrating on 'who' had a reason to kill her. It was a reasonable mistake to make, but a mistake nonetheless. Mrs Jeffries's only consolation was that they weren't the only ones concentrating on the wrong question. Inspector Witherspoon had made the same error.

Wiggins wasn't sure Mrs Jeffries was listening anymore. So he raised his voice and poked her lightly in the arm. 'And of course, I knew in me own mind that there was somethin' odd about the way it were all workin' out.'

Startled out of her thoughts, she flinched. 'Oh dear, I am sorry, Wiggins. I wasn't listening properly. I was thinking.' She stared at the lad and hoped she wasn't wrong. If she was, then what she was going to do might be utterly, utterly stupid. But her instincts were screaming that she was right, and as she was always admonishing the inspector to trust his instincts, she was going to do the same with hers.

'That's all right, Mrs Jeffries,' he replied affably. 'Sometimes my mind wanders too. Especially when Mrs Goodge or Betsy is lecturin' me about washing under me fingernails. Uh, what are you doin'?'

Mrs Jeffries grabbed his hand and jerked him towards the door. 'Hurry, Wiggins. We've not much time.' She pulled him towards the back stairs.

'Time for what?' he asked as he stumbled after her. 'Where are we goin'?'

'Upstairs,' she replied. 'We've got to get Smythe. You two have to get moving. The two of you need to get out of here right away.'

'You mean before the inspector comes home?' Wiggins asked eagerly. He loved going out on adventures.

'But shouldn't we wait so I can take Fred with me?' He especially loved adventures when he had his dog.

'Fred'll have to stay here,' she replied. 'We don't want the inspector to know you've gone out. I've got to talk to him before he goes to bed. I've got to tell him about Rollo Puffy. That's the only way this will work.'

'The only way what will work?' Wiggins asked breathlessly.

'My plan. We've got to plant the idea, Wiggins. Otherwise, a guilty woman will get away with murder. Twice.'

They'd reached the top landing. She dropped Wiggins's hand and dashed over to the door. She knocked. 'Smythe, do hurry. We need your help.'

Smythe was there in an instant. 'What's wrong? What's goin' on?'

She took a minute to catch her breath. Then she reached for the photograph that dangled from Wiggins's fingers. Holding it up, she said, 'The inspector is wrong. It wasn't Marlena McCabe that murdered Mirabelle Daws. It was this woman. Abigail Moulton. But we'll have to act quickly. I suspect she's not going to hang about much longer. You and Wiggins will have to move fast tonight.'

Smythe was rebuttoning the shirt he'd just unbuttoned as he listened. 'What do ya want us to do?'

''Tis a perfect day for a funeral,' Barnes said quietly. 'Gray, bleak and overcast. I don't think we'll be seein' the sun today, sir.'

Witherspoon nodded in agreement. He and the

constable were standing in Manor Park Cemetery. It was a good ways out of town, and both Barnes and the inspector had been rather surprised that the Prospers had chosen to bury a family member so far away from their home. It had taken the funeral party a good two hours to get here.

'I don't think they'll care.' He nodded towards the mourners who were standing around an open grave, less than a hundred feet away from them.

The hearse had pulled up a few feet from the grave, and the undertakers had taken out the plain, oak casket. A single wreath of daisies had been placed at the foot of the grave as the workmen solemnly lowered the coffin to its final resting place. A vicar stood at the head of the grave holding an open prayer book.

On the far side, Annabelle Daws Prosper, properly attired in black but wearing a chic hat without a veil, stood next to her husband. Mr Prosper held his wife's arm. His sister clung to his other arm. Her eyes were red rimmed, her hair untidy, but she was properly dressed in mourning black even though she'd never known the dead woman. Behind them, the servants stood solemnly, their expressions grim. Though whether it was sorrow for the victim they felt or pity for themselves for being dragged all the way out here was impossible to tell.

The vicar began the short graveside service.

Barnes glanced nervously about. He was reassured to see two constables staying discreetly back next to a large crypt.

'Not to worry, Constable,' Witherspoon reassured him. 'I don't think she'll make a run for it.'

218

'I'd not be too sure about that, sir,' Barnes replied. 'But if she does, we're ready. We've four constables stationed about the cemetery. That ought to be enough for one woman.'

'Excuse me, Inspector Witherspoon.' A familiar voice said from behind them.

Witherspoon and Barnes both whirled about and found themselves facing the purser from the *Island Star*. 'Good day, sirs.' The purser smiled broadly. He was a portly man with iron-gray hair and a cheerful countenance.

'Gracious,' the inspector said. 'It's Mr Faversham, isn't it? What are you doing here, sir?'

Tom Faversham's bright smile was replaced with a puzzled expression. 'What am I doing here? But you sent me a telegram. You said it was urgent that I come. I've come all the way up from Southampton on the morning train and then taken another train out here. This isn't an easy place to find, you know.'

'You received a telegram from me?' Witherspoon's brows drew together. 'I'm afraid there's been a mistake, sir. I did no such thing.'

'But the telegram said that if I didn't come, there would be a grave miscarriage of justice.' Tom Faversham pursed his lips. 'Do you think someone is having a joke at my expense, sir?'

'I expect so,' Barnes put in quickly. He didn't want to be distracted by a ship's purser if the McCabe woman tried to make a run for it. 'Too bad you've wasted your day, but as we've said, we didn't send a telegram. We are sorry you went to all the trouble of comin'.'

'A miscarriage of justice,' Witherspoon muttered. He didn't like the sound of that. For some odd reason, the story that his housekeeper had told him this morning popped into his head. Perhaps because she'd used the same words. He made a mental note to share the story with Constable Barnes. He'd find it quite amusing.

'It's all right, I suppose.' Faversham shrugged philosophically, his irritation vanishing as quickly as it had come. 'I wanted to come up to London anyway.'

'You're taking this quite well, sir,' Witherspoon said.

'Not really. I'd wanted to come to begin with, but Miss Annabelle, correction, Mrs Prosper, sent me that note saying the funeral was for family only. But seein' as how I'm here, I might as well go over and pay my respects to Miss Annabelle.'

Witherspoon looked over at the funeral party. The vicar had finished. He noticed that Annabelle Prosper had dropped her husband's arm.

'It looks like the service is finished,' Witherspoon said. 'You should have time to nip over before the family leaves. I'm sure Mrs Prosper, or as you knew her, Miss Annabelle, will appreciate your condolences.' From the corner of his eyes, he saw that the woman in question was staring at them, her attention focused on the purser.

Faversham started across the damp grass and then stopped suddenly. 'I'm too late. She must have already gotten into the carriage.'

Witherspoon pointed at Annabelle Prosper, who

was now backing away from the funeral party as fast as she could. 'She's right there.'

Bewildered, the purser shook his head. 'There's some mistake, Inspector. That woman isn't Annabelle Daws Prosper. It's Abigail Moulton.'

The woman gave up any pretense of subtley. She turned and bolted in the opposite direction.

Barnes looked frantically at his superior. He hadn't a clue what was going on, but something strange was happening. 'What should we do, sir?'

The funeral party gaped at the running woman. The two constables, who'd only been told to watch for a woman making a break for it, came bounding out from behind the crypt. They began the chase – she wouldn't get far. Their lives were filled with chasing fleeter-footed villains.

'After her,' the inspector called. He and Barnes took off at a run. Eldon Prosper, shouting his wife's name, bounded behind them. Marlena McCabe, who'd finally come out of her stupor to realize something rather peculiar was going on, went running after her brother. The Prosper servants, not knowing what else to do, took off after the rest of them.

The only people left standing at the grave site were the vicar, who was staring open-mouthed at the spectacle, and the undertaker's assistants, who weren't in the least surprised by the outburst. They'd seen plenty of strange goings-on at funerals.

Witherspoon and Barnes got there first. The woman was struggling hard, and the police constable, who was quite young and inexperienced, was turning a bright red as he tried to hang on to her without

221

either hurting her or touching body parts that were considered sacrosanct.

'Let me go, you great oaf,' she snapped.

'Let her go,' Witherspoon instructed. It was a safe instruction as they were now surrounded by police constables.

She yanked her arm out of the constable's grip and turned to glare at Inspector Witherspoon. 'I don't know what you think you're doing, but I'll have your job for this.'

'Are you Abigail Moulton?' he asked. But he knew in his heart that she was.

'Don't be absurd. I'm Annabelle Prosper.'

'You are not,' Tom Faversham interrupted. 'You're Abigail Moulton, and I can bring ten people here tomorrow to prove it. What have you done with Miss Annabelle? She got off the ship with you.'

'I don't know what you're talking about.'

'You know perfectly well what I'm on about,' Faversham cried. 'Where is she? Why isn't she here properly married to that Prosper fellow?'

The woman said nothing.

'Leave my wife alone,' Eldon Prosper ordered. He tried to break through the small circle of constables but couldn't. 'You've no right to handle her in such a fashion. No right at all. I'll have my solicitors on you, you can be sure of that.'

'I'm afraid your wife is under arrest,' Witherspoon replied.

'That's ridiculous,' Prosper charged. 'First you arrest my sister, and now you're trying to malign my wife. I'll not have it, I tell you. Annabelle, don't say a word to them. I'll bring Jackson to the station. We'll get this sorted out. You're not to worry about a thing, love. Not a thing.'

Witherspoon ignored him. 'Mrs Abigail Moulton, you're under the arrest for the murder of Mirabelle Daws and Annabelle Daws. Constable, please caution her and take her down to the station.'

Prosper protested the whole time they were leading her away. But in the end, he finally gave up and hurried off to get his solicitor.

'How did you know it was her?' Barnes asked as they walked back towards the grave site. 'I mean, how did you know what was going to happen?' He was rather awed by the quick turn of events. He knew his inspector was brilliant, but this was above and beyond anything he'd ever seen. 'I mean, uh, what did happen? Who's Abigail Moulton, and why would she want to murder Mirabelle Daws?'

Witherspoon sighed. 'It's rather a long story, Constable. Luckily, I had a little chat with my housekeeper last night. She filled me in on some gossip she'd heard about the Daws women.'

'I don't understand, sir,' Barnes said. 'How did you know something was goin' to happen today?'

'I didn't. But I think someone else did. Someone who badly wanted to see justice done in this case. I'll tell you all about it on the way back to the station.' He closed his eyes and briefly thanked heaven for housekeepers who couldn't sleep. 'I wouldn't have figured it out except that Mrs Jeffries told me the most amusing story. Remember that telegram I received giving us the identity of the dead woman?'

'Yes, sir, if we'd not got that telegram, that Mrs Moulton would have gotten away with murder. If we'd not found out the victim's identity, we'd never have solved this case.'

'Right,' Witherspoon agreed. 'Well, the telegram was signed by a fellow named Rollo Puffy. My house-keeper told me she'd remembered where she'd heard that name before. You recall that Mrs Jeffries used to be married to a police officer up in Yorkshire. He was always telling her tales he'd collected from all over the world. It seems that Rollo Puffy was once a rather rich eccentric in San Francisco. Then the name was used by quite a successful con artist. His specialty was pretending to be someone he wasn't.'

'That's remarkable, sir,' Barnes mumbled. He still didn't know what was going on or how the inspector had solved the case. Perhaps by the time they got back to the station, everything would begin to make sense.

They arrived back at the open grave. Witherspoon nodded politely to the vicar, knelt down and closed his eyes. Silently and earnestly he prayed for the soul of Mirabelle Daws.

'It was her, all right,' Wiggins said excitedly. 'You should 'ave seen it when she saw the purser comin' at 'er. She took off like a cat runnin' from the 'ounds.'

'It was a right strange sight,' Smythe agreed.

They were all gathered around the table at Upper Edmonton Gardens. Wiggins and Smythe, after a long and arduous night of rousting out witnesses, had hidden in the cemetery to watch the proceedings. They'd then nipped back to give their report.

'Seems to me you were lucky,' Luty snipped. She was out of sorts because it was Hatchet's photograph that had saved the day. 'What if that woman hadn't been Abigail Moulton? You'd have made a right fool of the inspector.'

'But we knew it were 'er,' Wiggins said eagerly. 'That's why we were up all night. We 'ad to nip down to Southampton lickety split, roust Mr Faversham and get 'im back up 'ere. But before he did his part at the cemetery, we stopped at Sheridan Square.' He stuffed a piece of ginger cake in his mouth.

'Can't you wait to feed your face until you finish telling us what happened?' Betsy cried.

'The lad's starved,' Smythe said. 'It was a long night. But like he said, we stopped at Sheridan Square and waited for the funeral party to leave the Prosper 'ouse. That's when Tom Faversham confirmed the woman were Abigail Moulton and not Annabelle Prosper.'

'Then you had him go on to the cemetery and pretend to get that telegram from the inspector?' Mrs Goodge was still a bit puzzled over the sequence of events. 'Is that right?'

'Right.' Smythe nodded. 'He was right 'appy to do it. Seems he liked the real Annabelle Prosper. When we explained what we thought might 'ave happened, he was keen to 'elp us.' The coachman didn't bother to tell them he'd paid the man fifty quid for his trouble.

Hatchet raised his teacup to Mrs Jeffries. 'Madam, I salute you for a brilliant piece of detective work.'

'I'll not take the credit for this one,' she said stoutly. 'All of you helped solve this puzzle.'

'I still don't know that I understand what happened,'

the cook cried. 'Why did Abigail Moulton kill Mirabelle Daws, and how come everyone thought she was Annabelle Daws?'

Mrs Jeffries smiled sympathetically. 'It is a complicated case because it really began when Annabelle came to England to many Eldon Prosper. As you told us, Mrs Goodge, Annabelle's former employer came on the ship with her. Abigail Moulton apparently realized that no one in England had ever seen Annabelle Daws. I think that she decided when they arrived here, rather than live as a disgraced widow and a poor relation, she'd take Annabelle's place. After all, she knew that Annabelle was coming here to marry a rich man and be the mistress of a fine house. Whereas she, disgraced by her husband's embezzlement and suicide, was going to have to go to the north of England and live with relatives who would probably make her life miserable. I suspect she decided to murder Annabelle before the ship even reached Southampton. She wanted to take her place.'

'But how could she?' Betsy asked. 'Surely Eldon Prosper would have realized the woman he'd married wasn't the woman he'd been corresponding with?'

'I imagine she had Annabelle's letters,' Mrs Jeffries replied.

'That stands to reason,' Luty said thoughtfully. 'Most women would hang on to the letters they got from the man they was fixin' to marry.'

'Remember, Annabelle had been her maid. She'd probably confided all manner of things to Abigail,' Hatchet added.

'Where would she get rid of the body?' Betsy asked.

'Oh, I imagine Annabelle Daws ended up in the Thames.' Mrs Jeffries shook her head sadly. 'Poor woman never had a chance. Then, of course, when Abigail got the letter from Mirabelle saying she was coming for a visit, she knew her masquerade would be exposed. She had to kill Mirabelle. So she sent her a message to meet her in the garden early in the morning. I'm sure she knew about Mirabelle's concern for her. Mirabelle made no secret of the fact that she thought something was wrong at the Prosper household.'

'So she sends her a mysterious note.' Luty picked up the thought. 'And then lies in wait for her out in the garden. But how on earth did she think she'd not get caught? A dead woman in a posh place like Sheridan Square is goin' to raise a fuss.'

'That's true,' Mrs Jeffries agreed. 'But the fuss would die down when the dead woman wasn't identified. That's what she was counting on. That no one would know that it was Mirabelle Daws who was the victim. She'd not realized that both her husband and her sister-in-law knew about Mirabelle's visit and had reasons of their own to fear it.'

'What did she do with Mirabelle's things?' Wiggins asked.

'I'm not sure,' the housekeeper said, 'but I've a feeling that if the police search that empty house on Sheridan Square, they'll not only find Mirabelle's things, but perhaps Annabelle's as well. We had a report that noises had been heard in that place.'

'I still think it's remarkable that you put it all together, madam,' Hatchet said.

'Not really,' Mrs Jeffries said. 'Actually, once Luty told us the story of Rollo Puffy and then Wiggins identifed the woman in the photograph, it was simple. After that, everything made sense. The fact that Mrs Prosper wouldn't respond to her sister's letters, those sudden hysterics at the mortuary . . .'

'What about 'em?' Luty asked.

'Remember, the inspector said she was quite calm until they started into the viewing room. Then she suddenly threw herself in her husband's arms and got hysterical. But she did it just as the purser, who knew her as Abigail Moulton, was coming out of that very room. She didn't want him to see her, and she had to act fast. I think what really set it in my own mind was when Wiggins said she'd sent the purser a note telling him not to attend the funeral service. That was simply out of character for someone of Annabelle's background.'

'What about Mrs McCabe and the necklace?' Hatchet asked.

'I think she's telling the truth, or at least a part of it.'

'I think she spotted Mirabelle arrivin',' Mrs Goodge put in. 'Remember, she was the one that heard the hansom cab arrive that morning and saw Mirabelle get out. I think she waited a bit to go out to the garden, not knowing exactly why Mirabelle was there, and then when she did go out, she saw the woman had been stabbed. So she took the necklace and ran.'

'But why didn't she tell the police?' Betsy asked.

'Because she thought her brother 'ad done the killin',' Smythe said softly. 'Remember, Fiona told

Wiggins she'd seen Prosper that night. Probably Mrs McCabe 'ad seen 'im too, and she didn't know that her sister-in-law wasn't Annabelle, so she didn't think she'd have a reason to murder the woman. Stands to reason she'd think it was her brother.'

Mrs Jeffries nodded in agreement. 'You're right, Smythe. I do believe that's how it must have happened.'

'How did you convince the inspector to go along?' Luty asked.

'I didn't.' Mrs Jeffries laughed. 'I merely planted a few seeds last night when the inspector got home.' She nodded appreciatively at the cook. 'It's amazing how useful a bit of gossip turns out to be.'

The inspector arrived home quite late that evening. He insisted on eating in the kitchen, rather than have the staff go to the trouble of bringing his dinner to the dining room.

'I say, this soup is excellent.' He smiled appreciatively at the cook.

'Thank you, sir,' Mrs Goodge replied. 'I thought you might be hungry, sir. Mrs Jeffries told us you'd had quite an eventful day.'

He had given the housekeeper a brief synopsis when he was hanging up his coat and hat.

'Indeed it has been eventful,' he replied. 'And it looks as if it's going to be a long and arduous trial. Mrs Prosper is being represented by one of the best legal firms in England.'

'How can she afford that?' Wiggins asked. He was helping Mrs Jeffries put the copper pot on the top shelf of the pine bureau.

'She can't, but her husband can,' he said. 'Eldon Prosper has plenty of money. Our task is not going to be an easy one. Not only must we prove that she murdered Mirabelle Daws, but that she murdered Annabelle as well.'

'You mean that Mr Prosper is still goin' to help the woman, knowin' that she killed 'is real fiancée?' Wiggins was shocked.

'I'm afraid so,' Witherspoon sighed. 'He told me he didn't care who the woman was; she was his wife, and he loved her. He's going to do whatever he can to save her. Well, he might be able to save her from hanging, but I don't think he'll save her from prison. Even without Annabelle's body, we've a strong case against her.' He suddenly looked around the kitchen. 'I say, where are Smythe and Betsy?'

'They're out in the garden, sir,' Mrs Jeffries replied. She brushed the dust off her hands and came towards the table. 'As a matter of fact, I believe I hear them coming now.' She had a strong feeling that an announcement of some kind might be in the offing.

A moment later, the two of them came into the kitchen. They were holding hands.

Mrs Goodge looked knowingly at Mrs Jeffries.

'Good evening, Smythe, Betsy.' Witherspoon beamed at the two of them. Then he noticed their entwined fingers. 'Oh dear, dear me. Smythe, do you really think you ought to be doing that?'

'I do, sir.' Smythe grinned wickedly. 'I'm glad everyone's 'ere. Betsy and I 'ave something to tell ya all.' He looked at the maid. 'Do ya want me to say it?'

Suddenly, shy, she nodded. 'Go on, then.'

He took a deep breath. 'Betsy has done me the great honor of agreein'...'

'To get engaged,' Betsy interrupted. 'That's what we've agreed. We're going to be engaged.'

'Gracious, how very wonderful,' the inspector enthused. 'I'm so pleased for the both of you.'

'Congratulations,' Mrs Jeffries said. She smiled broadly, delighted her intution had been on the mark. 'I know the two of you will be happy. I think you're perfect for one another.'

'Cor blimey,' Wiggins cried. 'It's about time.'

'All the best to both of you,' Mrs Goodge added. 'But you should have said something. I'd have made a special dinner for you. So when's the wedding to be?'

'Thank you, everyone,' Betsy said. She gave her intended a fast, quick smile. 'We haven't set a date yet.'

Smythe, who seemed to be in a state of shock, simply stared at her.

It took a moment or two before Mrs Jeffries realized that it wasn't simply a matter of the man being lovestruck. He really had been surprised.

'As a matter of fact.' Betsy grabbed Smythe's hand. 'We'd best go back outside and talk a bit more.' She began tugging him toward the back hall. 'We'll be right back.'

As soon as they'd disappeared, Inspector Witherspoon looked at Mrs Jeffries. 'I say, did you notice that Smythe seemed to be a bit stunned?'

'Oh, that's normal, sir,' Mrs Jeffries replied. 'All men act stunned when they realize they've actually gotten engaged.'

'What are you playin' at?' Smythe hissed at Betsy as soon as they were out of earshot. 'If ya don't want to marry me, all ya had to do was say so.'

'Don't be daft,' she whispered. She reached for the back door, yanked it open and jerked him outside. 'Of course I want to marry you. But I suddenly realized what we were about to do.'

Smythe glared at her. 'What are you goin' on about? We were about to tell the others we wanted to be married.'

'Right,' she agreed, 'and then you were goin' to tell them you were rich.'

'So? Why shouldn't I tell 'em the truth? I'm right tired of livin' a lie, Betsy.'

'I don't doubt it,' she replied. 'But think a minute. Where would that leave us? I'll tell you where we'd be. Living all on our own in some big fancy house without any murders to investigate, that's where. Are you ready to give it up?'

He frowned thoughtfully. 'Why would we have to give up our investigatin'?'

'We wouldn't have to,' Betsy said, 'but you know as well as I do that it would be different. Oh, maybe not at first, but eventually things would start to change and before you knew it, we'd be too busy with our own lives to want to do any snooping about. Look, Smythe, you know I love you more than anything. But our investigations has made me feel right important. Like I'm contributing something to this world that only I can give . . . oh, I don't think I know how to explain it, but I know I'm not ready to give it up.

Not yet. I don't want things to change. I'm not ready for it.'

'I think I know what you're sayin',' he agreed slowly. 'But how long exactly are ya thinkin' we ought to be engaged?'

'Not too long,' Betsy said, delighted that he wasn't going to give her too much trouble. 'Maybe a year or two. Just long enough for us to get some idea about how we'd be a part of things once we was married and livin' on our own.'

Smythe was silent for a moment. 'I guess you're right,' he finally said. 'I'm not ready to give up our investigatin' either, and once we was married, we would want our own place. All right, then, we'll be engaged for a bit. But just long enough to suss out how we're goin' to do things once we're married.'

Betsy decided that was probably about as good a compromise as she was likely to get. She slipped her arms around his neck. 'I'm so glad you understand, Smythe.'

He pulled her close. At least, he thought, now that they were officially engaged, she'd be much easier to handle.

She smiled up at him. Now that they were engaged, she thought, he'd be so much easier to handle.